Rocky Mountain Challenge

C. R. Fulton

THE CAMPGROUND KIDS
www.bakkenbooks.com

Rocky Mountain Challenge by C. R. Fulton
Copyright © 2022 C.R. Fulton

Cover Credit: Anderson Design Group, Inc.

All rights reserved. This book is protected under the copyright laws of the United States of America. This book may not be copied or reprinted for commercial gain or profit.

ISBN 978-1-955657-35-8
For Worldwide Distribution
Printed in the U.S.A.

Published by Bakken Books
2022

*To every adventurer,
whether in body or mind,
always run toward the light
and leave the shadows behind you!*

The Campground Kids

No. 1
Grand Teton Stampede

No. 2
Smoky Mountain Survival

No. 3
Zion Gold Rush

No. 4
Rocky Mountain Challenge

No. 5
Grand Canyon Rescue

For more books, check out:
www.bakkenbooks.com

- 1 -

Monday

I fold my arms, holding them close to my chest, as I prepare to fall backward into thin air. *I can do this. Just let go, then everyone will catch me.* That's what a "trust fall" is—knowing everyone else is there. Except, I'm the first one doing it, so I'm not even positive this team-building exercise will really work.

I roll my shoulders; all the pushups and lifting weights have added muscle to my sturdy, almost 13-year-old frame. But muscle is not an asset—not when I might crash through everyone's arms and into the ground.

"Isaiah Rawlings, keep your body straight and fall back," encourages Jim, my wilderness survival training week counselor.

Opening my eyes, I look over my shoulder. Two rows of kids face each other, their arms outstretched, making a bed of sorts. I shouldn't have looked. Climbing high on the huge stump hadn't bothered me at all, but now sweat breaks out on my upper lip.

Sadie, my sister, is there waiting. She just turned ten, and we've been on a lot of adventures together. I wish the entire group were made up of Sadie repeats. The thought makes me smile. *What if all 12 Sadie clones ate sugar at once?* The world surely couldn't handle that much raw energy!

I shift my foot back, teetering as my heel slides off the edge. I bite my lip. My 14-year-old cousin Ethan is there too. I remember his shouting for help as the river in the Grand Tetons had sucked him away. *He'll be there to help catch me.*

Jim clears his throat. Standing here thinking is

only making the exercise worse. This is why we applied for this six-day camp tucked right along the border of the Rocky Mountain National Park—to train and then employ what we learn. I've been longing for this Monday to come!

I release a slow breath. *Three…Two…One…* I fall backward stiffly, my mind empty, with only the whoosh of air in my ears. A heartbeat passes, then another, and I land safely in the cradle-like embrace of 12 sets of arms.

My eyes snap open, and Jim yells a whoop of congratulations. I feel almost weightless as I'm lowered to my feet. I can't wipe the grin off my face, with everyone's clapping and cheering.

Jim nods when Sadie cries, "Me next!" I take her place below the tall stump, and we hold out our arms. Sadie's slim figure barely hesitates before she falls backward, her long, brown ponytail whipping straight up, and I'm shocked at how easy it is to catch her. I guess I didn't need to worry about being too heavy. When the load is spread out, it's easy.

Soon, the other boys from my cabin have completed the trust fall. There's Aaron, his dark skin glistening in the heat. Then redheaded Dan, whose freckles look like sand sprinkled over his nose.

Aaron's sister, Zenya, goes next. Even though we only arrived at camp two hours ago, she and Sadie are already best friends. Then Miguel, with his straight black hair and wide smile, shouts as he falls. Finally, it's Ethan's turn. He stands atop the stump, staring down at us. He looks even taller up there, with his long thin arms, his trim hips, and his shaggy hair waving in the breeze.

"Um…Ethan? You're supposed to turn around," I say flatly.

He shakes his head. "Nope," he declares.

"Uh, yes, you are," Sadie adds.

Ethan climbs off the stump, and Jim walks over from another group also doing trust falls.

"Ethan, hang on now. Let's give it a minute! You know how easy it was to catch everyone else; you can do this." Jim is tall and well-built, a confident

20 year old. I guess he's just about what every boy here wishes he could be someday.

"*Au contraire,* sir," Ethan replies. "You do not know my luck."

"That's true, but I do know about survival; and in 99 out of 100 situations, teamwork is what helps you survive. That's why we kick off this camp with the trust fall."

Ethan wrinkles one side of his nose. "I don't mind teamwork, but I do mind…well, I'm just not going to do it."

Jim nods. "Okay, but remember, every activity counts toward your final score at the awards ceremony on Saturday."

I can hardly believe we're here—with six days of intense training and fun ahead of us. When we applied, it seemed as if we would never hear that our applications had been accepted. Sadie, Ethan, and I had barely enough camping hours to meet the minimum requirement to attend.

"All right, you've got 15 minutes of break time

to get settled in your assigned cabins. Then we will meet under the bell," Jim says loud enough for the entire group of 24 kids to hear.

"So, what's the bell for?" I ask.

Jim shrugs. "In all my years at Camp Wilderness, I've only heard that emergency bell ring once."

I nod and run to catch up with Ethan, Aaron, Dan, and Miguel.

"Yeah, it ought to go like…Cabin 3 will bring them to their knees…" Aaron pumps his arms in the air as he chants, "The competition's done because the Cabin 3 boys won!"

Dan's red hair glints in the sunlight.

Ethan repeats the chant altogether, beatboxing between the sentences, and I must admit, it sounds cool.

"This year we're going to be the high-point cabin," Miguel says with quiet confidence.

"Stop!" My sudden, harsh whisper makes our entire group freeze.

… # -2-

I point ahead of us toward the trees in front of Cabin 3. "See?" There's a brief blur of movement low to the ground.
"It's a cougar!" Aaron leaps behind me.
I shake my head, unsure. Whatever the creature was, it seems to have disappeared into thin air.
"It was huge!" Aaron declares.
"Things are almost never as big as you remember. Maybe we can find the tracks!" I rush forward, searching among the pine needles and aspen leaves.
"Here!" Ethan is kneeling next to a sandy spot. We gather around and study a clear print.

"I don't see any claw marks, and the heel pad is large. It must have been some sort of cat!" I say, recalling my well-studied tracking book.

"Told you!" Aaron's bright white teeth stand out against his skin.

"Well, I, for one, am heading in for a snack." Ethan is the tallest kid at camp, and it seems like he never stops eating.

"Did you bring any cookies?" I ask, recalling the depth of his affection for them at Zion National Park this summer.

"Nope, I thought Twizzlers would be harder for creatures to steal."

We clump up the wooden steps to the cabin, and I pull out a piece of the deer jerky that Aunt Sylvia had given me.

"Oohh! Can I have some?" Ethan asks.

"Didn't your mom give you a pound of it too?" I've been carefully planning the rationing of this high-protein snack to last all week.

"I ate it already."

"On the drive here?" I look at him in disbelief. It had taken Mom two days to drive us here. *That's half a pound a day!* Ethan only belches in reply as he settles a coonskin cap on his head. I pick out a small piece of jerky and hand it to him.

"Look at this," Aaron says.

We all gather around to see his watch with a built-in compass. "My sister has one too, but she doesn't know how to use it." He slaps his leg, laughing.

"That compass will come in handy on Wednesday—maps and tracking day." I pull more supplies from my pack and slip them into my pocket. *You can never be too prepared.*

I can't believe I'm finally here! Mom's writing conference is two towns to the east, and that's how she found out about the special camping week. Dad will be here for Saturday, the big competition and awards day.

"Come on, let's get back to the bell. I wouldn't want to miss out on our first chance to beat Cabin 5," Aaron calls.

We rush out the door.

I study the trees, but there's no flash of tan fur this time. "Isn't that the girls' cabin?"

"Yeah! I can beat my sister any day. But you heard Jim say since there are only four girls total at camp, Cabin 5 will have a handicap—you know, extra free points since they don't have a fifth person. I think giving them points stinks."

"Well, they have fewer people, so it only seems fair to me. Unless you want to compete on their team!" I add, simply because I don't like how eager he is to beat everyone.

"*Waugh!*" Aaron falls to the ground. "I would rather die!" He's on his feet again in a flash. "Come on, hurry!"

We run the rest of the way to the bell and arrive out of breath.

"All right, survivalists! Listen up. Every cabin is a team. Every activity your cabin completes this week will receive a score, and this first set of games will help us counselors see and become accustomed to your capabilities. This camp will be an intense six days with plenty of opportunities for injury. So, we need to know each of your strengths and weaknesses." Jim blows a whistle. "Line up between the flags by the main lodge."

We rush over, and I'm glad to see Sadie's counselor is a slim, sweet-faced blonde. Sadie had been worried about spending so many nights away from Mom and Dad; but she's smiling now, obviously telling her counselor a story.

I slip into the middle of our group, where my slower running won't lose the relay race for us. I'm built for strength, not speed, and I'm okay with that weak point. Aaron steps to the back of the line, bouncing eagerly on his toes.

I study the four teams of guys. The Cabin 2 guys look like they will bring us some pretty stiff competition.

Jim hands out a red baton to each team. Ethan drops to one knee, digging the toe of his shoe into the grass as my heart begins to pound.

"Ready, set, go!" Jim shouts, and the runners take off for the flag at the far end of the field. Ethan's shirt is plastered to his slim form as his long legs eat up the distance. Midway, his coonskin cap flies off. The girls must wait until the first two runners get back to start their race.

"Run!" I shout, caught up in the excitement.

Ethan slaps the baton into Miguel's outstretched hand and falls to the ground. All he can do is gasp for breath. All too soon Miguel is back, and I tuck my head and run for all I'm worth. The Cabin 2 runner passes me.

I skid around the flag and stretch my stride as far as it will go, my legs feeling like lead. I pass the baton and watch Dan's lightning speed recover first place. He comes in just ahead of the Cabin 2 guy, and the team runner for the girls' cabin is right with him.

It seems as if Aaron has been shot from a cannon, but Sadie is the last runner for Cabin 5; I see she's not going to give him a break. The two of them outpace the Cabin 2 runner, and I'm shouting like crazy, jumping up and down. Neck and neck, Sadie and Aaron take the far turn. Then Aaron finds another gear, and he pulls ahead for the win! We jump, shaking each other and cheering.

"You girls didn't stand a chance!" Aaron shouts.

Zenya's hair is tightly braided. As she shifts her head to one side, her attitude is easy to see. "Whatever! You better watch out next time," she fires back at him.

Sadie is breathing too hard to say anything, and I wish I could tell her what an excellent job she did. However, the counselors direct us toward an obstacle course. On the way, Ethan scoops up his cap. We study the walls and pits ahead of us.

"We got this! We had a great start. Let's keep it up, Cabin 3!" *Aaron might be a bit too competitive.*

"First thing to know about this course is…your entire team must cross the goal line to finish at all. Remember, in survival situations, your life might depend on the people you're with and how well you can work together. Not everything is as it seems on this course, so put on your thinking caps and do not leave a teammate behind!"

Jim counts down again, and we rush forward to the first wooden wall. It's about as high as my chest, and I enjoy the ease of my muscles taking me over it. The walls we must scale gradually get higher. When we reach the third one, try as he might, even Ethan's height can't conquer it.

"Guys!" I exclaim. They finally turn to me from their futile efforts. "Remember? Jim said we would need to work as a team." I link my fingers together like a step. "Ethan, up and over!"

His shoe bites into the skin of my hands, and I grimace as I heft him up to the top. Finally, he gets an elbow over, and his weight lifts off my hands.

Aaron is trying to boost Dan over without success. Ethan is hanging over the top, helping Miguel climb up. I take a quick glance at the other teams. The Cabin 2 team is still throwing themselves at the wall, trying to get up on their own.

Zenya is the tallest girl, and I notice her bent-over position with her hands gripping her knees. The others from her cabin are using her back as a step!

Soon, I'm the only one on my team left on this side of the wall, and my stomach muscles are burning like crazy from the strain. The other boys must be holding Ethan's legs because he is dangling over the wall, reaching far down for me. I leap for his hands and groan as I struggle upward, my grip slipping till I finally land on top of the wall and slide over.

"What's next?" I pant. Out of the corner of my eye, I catch sight of the girls pulling Zenya over the top of their wall.

"Simple! Monkey bars!" Aaron takes off for our cabin's set of bars, leaping high. He swings easily; but as soon as the third rung takes his weight, it pops loose, and he crashes to the ground.

"Hey!" His pride is battered more than anything else. "This thing must be as old as the hills!"

Beside us, Zenya does a repeat of Aaron's performance, except she lands on her feet, holding the third rung in her hands.

Jim grins wide. "No feet on the ground, teams! You must make it across without touching the ground. Think it through. These monkey bars are not old—just tricky."

I study the outside bars farther down. "Wait! There aren't any rungs at all toward the middle!"

Jim crosses his arms, nodding. "Surviving isn't always clear-cut; life can throw curveballs at you."

"Let me see that," I say, studying the rung that had let loose on Aaron. "There aren't any screw holes in this rung! It didn't break; it wasn't ever connected in the first place!"

The first team member from Cabin 2 swings onto the third bar, and we watch him fall to the ground. Chewing the inside of my lip, I formulate a plan. "Who's the best at balancing?"

Dan steps forward and says, "I am." I do not detect any pride in his claim.

"Okay, you need to get on top and hold down the loose rungs. Then you need to move the loose rungs forward to fill the empty spaces so the rest of us can cross."

Dan struggles up the slick post, so I give him a boost, handing up the rung once he balances on top of the bars.

"Miguel, you first," Dan says, settling the bar into its spot.

He holds it until Miguel is safely past. Then he slides forward on the wide horizontal beams to the empty spot Miguel is now dangling in front of.

"Hurry!" Miguel's voice sounds pinched as his fingers begin to slip.

Dan sets the bar into the new spot. "Go!"

I feel relieved when Miguel lands solidly on the far side. Jim nods at me. "Nice idea, Rawlings."

"Thanks," I reply, but a glance at the girls reveals they've copied my idea, and they're getting ahead of our team.

"Come on, Isaiah," Dan urges.

I leap for the first bar. Being big-boned and heavier than most boys my age makes traversing the monkey bars the most difficult playground equipment for me to master. Right now, with my fingers slipping as I wait for Dan to move the bar, I growl, determined not to fall.

He slams the bar into place. I swing my legs, fingers barely reaching it, then I hit the ground on the far side. The entire girls' team is already racing toward the last obstacle.

"What? No fair! They all crossed over the top!" Ethan cries, dangling by one hand from the bars right behind me.

Jim shrugs. "The only rule was not to touch the ground. Survival in the wild means you must think creatively—outside the box."

The girls' counselor is clapping as they race forward.

With a groan of frustration, Aaron shimmies up the post and crosses over the top; in seconds, he and Dan are with us.

We break forward with the Cabin 2 team only steps behind. A quick glance over my shoulder reveals the other teams are also closing in. They didn't have to stop to figure out a strategy; they simply copied ours! I swallow down the frustration, nearly plowing into Ethan.

"What?" I ask.

-3-

My team is staring open-mouthed at the last obstacle. A deep ditch looks freshly dug with an excavator. The finish sign is posted on the other side of the ditch!

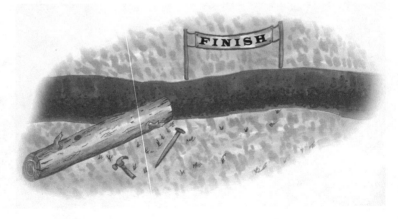

"This ditch is half a mile deep," Jim announces through a megaphone.

"No, it isn't," Zenya contradicts him. As usual, her one hand rests on her hip.

"For the purpose of this exercise, young lady, it is! Anyone who falls in must restart the obstacle. I repeat, no one may touch the ditch. Now go!"

A strange assortment of items has been piled in front of each team. I see a log with a two-inch hole drilled through it, a long metal pole, and a hammer. The Cabin 2 team jumps into action, pushing their log forward, trying to force it to span the wide ditch. The heavy wood promptly dives into the canyon, digging into the rich brown dirt at an angle.

"Oh, no!" their team counselor groans. "The penalty for losing your bridge is harsh!" He and Jim wrestle the log out of the ditch and push it even farther away than it had been the first time. The Cabin 2 guys moan.

"Okay, so, the log is how we're supposed to cross the ditch. He called it a *bridge*," I say.

"Right, but how do we do it?" Aaron's face has turned a reddish hue, his competitive spirit is pushing him hard.

"Why don't we try rolling it really fast?" Ethan suggests.

"No way! The log will just roll down into the canyon really fast." The Cabin 4 team proves my point as they try that exact suggestion. Their bridge ends up at the bottom, and the counselors struggle to drag it back. The boys of Cabin 2 are red-faced as they struggle to push their bridge closer to the chasm once again.

I pluck at my lip, thinking hard. I notice the hole in the log is just the right size for the pole to fit through. And now that I take a careful look, I see the hole in the log isn't in the center of its length; it's fairly close to one end. A quick check confirms my suspicion; each log is drilled the same way.

"Wait!" I snap my fingers. "The log is designed to be a pivot!"

"A *what?*" Dan and Ethan ask at the same time.

"Come on!" I motion everyone to come closer and lower my voice. "If we put the pipe through the hole, hammer the pole into the ground, we could push the opposite end of the log and pivot it over the open space to the other side."

"Now, why didn't I think of that?" Ethan says.

Dan's red hair glints in the sun. "We'll need weight on this end of the log while we swing it, or the weight of the log will pull out the stake."

"Okay, we must work fast! Everyone else will catch on quick," I say.

Aaron puts his fist in the center of our huddle, and we set ours on top. "Cabin 3!" he shouts, and we mime an explosion with our hands as we spin into action.

Ethan scoops up the pipe, and Aaron guides it into the hole in the log. The hammer is in my hand even though I don't remember picking it up. Dan and Miguel shove the log close to the edge of the ditch, then hold it steady as I climb on and lift the hammer high.

The loud ping of metal-on-metal rings loud, and I grimace. The rocky ground resists my blows to pound the pipe deep into the earth. Sweat is rolling between my shoulder blades as I hop down.

"Let's spin it!" I drop the hammer and start to push the log.

"Wait!" Dan shouts, as the long end of the log slowly eases over the chasm. "It's tipping!" He leaps onto the short end near the pipe—the same end that I'm pushing on.

"How are we supposed to move it with you on it?" Aaron's voice is pinched as we hear each of the other teams pounding their pipe with their hammer. "They're right behind us! They stole our idea, so we have to win!"

"We'll work together. Everybody, watch the log and keep it level. We will add more weight as we swing the bridge over the gully," says Ethan.

Ethan is right. The only way to make this exercise successful is to work together as a team.

Ignoring the urge to look at the others, we focus

on inching the log bridge out over the chasm. Once again the log starts to dip downward.

"We need more weight!" Miguel shouts as the log starts to dip down. Grunting and sweating, we make what seems like a thousand adjustments, and the bridge finally settles on the other side!

"Yes!" Aaron's fist beats the air as he leaps onto the log and scurries across. Dan and Miguel join him, and then Ethan darts forward. Halfway there, a bumblebee's erratic flight connects hard with the back of Ethan's head.

He screams, smacking at his shaggy hair, and his feet tangle up. As he goes down, his stomach catches the log, and he desperately wraps his long arms around it.

"Help!" he screeches. "I'm going to fall!"

I roll my eyes as he kicks his long legs wildly. "Ethan!" I shout. "Just fall and get it over with."

"Nooooo!" he shouts dramatically as his grip finally fails. He drops about six inches to the ground. He pats himself down and quips, "Oh, I survived!"

I shake my head at him and help him out of the ditch. "You weren't supposed to fall."

"A kamikaze bumblebee assaulted me. His attack was unprovoked, mind you!"

"Sure," I agree, following him across the log. Aaron, Dan, Miguel, and Ethan rush over the finish line. A few steps from it, I turn to see Cabin 4 had tried our plan without pounding the spike deep enough into the ground. Currently, the counselors are once again hauling out their log.

The other teams aren't faring any better. Cabin 2 is trying to force the log across without the spike since they couldn't get it driven into the hard ground. The log crashes into the canyon again.

Sadie is pounding as hard as she can, but she hands off the hammer to the next girl. Then she shakes out her wrists as if they hurt. *Now that I think about it, using that hammer did sting my hand when the metal connected.*

"Come on, Isaiah!" Aaron is freaking out, pointing at the finish line.

"I'll be right back," I say.

Aaron falls to the ground, clutching his head, but I jet across our sturdy bridge and over to the girls.

"Here…" I hold out my hand for the hammer that Zenya is holding.

"Why would *you* help us?" she asks, her head weaving from side to side.

"What are you doing, Rawlings?" Dan shouts, but I ignore him.

I look at Zenya and reply, "Because my sister gave this course her best effort, she deserves to cross the finish line too."

Sadie smiles at me. Zenya casts a confused look between Sadie and me as she hands me the tool. On my first hammer stroke, I discover that they had hit a rock. Grimacing, I wind up with everything I have, stomach clenched tight, and slam down the hammer. I feel the concussion all the way to my shoulders, but the pole inches downward. *It must have broken through!* After that first strike, the rod drives in more easily.

C. R. Fulton

"Thanks, Bud," Sadie says as I hop off the log.

I wave at her, then spread my arms for balance as I cross our bridge again. Jim is waiting under the finish line with a look of pleased surprise on his face. I think he's the only one who's happy to see me.

"How could you do that to our team?" asks Aaron with a disapproving tone as I step over the line.

"The other teams are way behind; we were guaranteed to win."

-4-

By the time we're back in the main fields for the fire-starting lesson, most of my team has forgiven me, *I think.*

"So, what do a cotton ball, some ashes, and flat pieces of wood equal?" Jim asks.

"A bad joke!" Ethan quips, slapping his knee.

Jim laughs easily. "No, *fire.*"

"What?" Ethan's nose wrinkles up on one side.

"Oh…um, wait! I know this," Zenya snaps her fingers, as she tries to recall the answer. "That's called…a fire roll! Right?"

"Yep! Have you made one before?" asks Caroline, the girls' counselor.

Zenya shakes her head.

"Well, there's no time like the present to learn," Caroline says.

As Ethan plucks a cotton ball out of the bag, he asks, "Why do bees have sticky hair?"

Clearly his fall from the log is fresh in his mind.

"Bees don't have hair," Zenya says.

"Lots of bees do," Sadie corrects her.

"Because they use honeycombs!" Ethan quips.

Dan laughs so hard, he snorts; then Miguel joins him.

"I cannot believe someone finally laughed at a joke of yours," Sadie says.

"Miracles happen," Ethan replies happily.

"Here's another miracle for you—one that might save your life someday." Jim interrupts as he rips a short strip of cotton from a small ball. Then he pours a bit of cold ash from a bottle onto it and rolls the cotton up tight between his palms until it is shaped like a cocoon and even looks much like one.

"Well, where do we get the spark?" Sadie asks.

"That's the thing about a fire roll. You don't need a spark." Jim takes the now-grayish-colored cotton and places it on a flat piece of wood and sprinkles more ash over everything. He takes the other piece of wood and rubs the roll quickly between them.

This method of starting a fire could take a while—like starting a friction fire.

"And…we have smoke!" Jim announces. The look of accomplishment on Jim's face shows how much he loves all things outdoors.

"Already?" Ethan clearly had the same thoughts as I had.

Jim carefully pulls the now tightly rolled cotton free of the wood, and I'm shocked to see a tendril of smoke rising from it. Jim cradles it with more cotton balls and soon a red glow flares up, igniting the larger pieces of cotton. He sets them down and crushes pine needles between his palms, crumbling them on top of the smoking fire roll. Seconds later, the needles burst into strong flames.

"Wow! I thought you could only light a fire that

quickly with some lighter fluid and a striker," Dan comments.

"Tonight, we are cooking our dinner over a bonfire. Problem is, we have no fire yet," Jim says as he stomps out his fire roll.

"Let me at it. I'll build you the best bonfire ever," Ethan boasts, taking some supplies from Jim.

The counselors hand out sets of material to each camper, so they can all learn this new method of starting a fire. Ethan soon discovers that Jim had made it look easy.

"Umm, so…fasting isn't that bad, right?" Ethan asks, frowning at the random bits of smashed cotton after he rubs his fire roll between the two pieces of wood.

"Ethan, you must press the wood together hard. Try again! I don't want to hear you whine about how hungry you are," Jim says with a smirk.

Miguel is the first one to get smoke from the cotton and cold ashes. Ethan doubles his pace as he rubs a new roll between the wood.

"*Wahoo!*" he shouts, carefully picking up the cotton and cradling it exactly as Jim had. "Oh, rock-a-bye flames..." He rocks the cotton against his chest. "Ouch!" Ethan nearly throws the wad into the grass. As he fumbles his fire roll from hand to hand, he continues to sing "...on the treetop..." Unexpectedly, the cotton bursts into flames... "Ouch! All right, so you want pine needles—not a treetop!" he says to the glowing embers. He drops the cotton into the fire ring, tucking pine needles on top, sucking his overheated finger.

"See, what did I tell you?" he exclaims, way too proud of his sputtering flames.

I sniff; a tiny wisp of smoke is rising from my board too.

"Wow!" I whisper as I pull the roll free. *Fire* is such an important part of staying alive in the wilderness. Creating it with just a few plant fibers, ashes, and wood brings me a deep sense of security inside. Now I know one more secret of the universe. I add my small flame to the ring.

"Does it only work with cotton?" Sadie asks, as she sets her roll next to mine. We feed the tiny flames licking at the cotton rolls, add some pine needles and then small twigs.

"You can use any dry, fluffy plant material. Cattails work great when their tops are fuzzy," Caroline answers.

In a few minutes, a nice, cheery bonfire is burning bright. With their stomachs growling, the campers load hotdogs on long sticks to roast.

I watch the flames lick up the wood, growing brighter by the second as the sun goes down on our first day of survival training camp.

I lose track of how many hotdogs I roast and eat as Jim teaches us more about fire craft. I notice the glow makes his skin look like bronze.

"This week we'll be training you in the five basic survival skills that make it possible to live in almost any environment. Skill one involves mastering fire. We'll work on becoming proficient in this skill throughout the week because fire is the king of all survival tools! Tonight, y'all did great! The other four skills we will be learning include building a shelter, signaling, finding food and water, and lastly, applying first aid.

"We'll work on each skill for one day. Then on Saturday, we'll hold our final competitions for the week. At the conclusion, we will have an awards ceremony. Your parents will be here on that day, so you will have the opportunity to show off all the skills you have learned this week. But never forget, teamwork is essential to survival. Being able to trust everyone around you is key. Even more important is being trustworthy yourself."

In the firelight, with the faces of so many new friends around me, Jim's words about teamwork and trust settle deep inside me.

-5-

"WHAT HAPPENED IN HERE?" Ethan's sharp cry makes me hurry up the steps.

My jaw drops as I survey the interior of our small cabin. Our clothes and shoes have been thrown everywhere.

"Looks like a dozen coffee-drinking squirrels had a party in here!" he whispers, his voice cracking the way it has been lately—first too high, then too low.

I can't even begin to formulate a logical response to his absolutely absurd statement as the boys push us forward.

"Aw, man!" Aaron shrieks in disgust.

Jim steps inside. "Whoa! Any idea what happened, boys?"

"Yeah," Aaron says, pounding his fist into his palm. "It's called the G-I-R-L-S."

"*Hmm.*" Jim's voice rumbles deep in his chest, and I wonder when Ethan's will sound like that. "Was the door open?"

"Yeah, it was open when I came up to it," Ethan whispers, still in shock.

"Well, let's do our best to pick up for now. You can do a better job tomorrow," Jim says.

Aaron is still pounding his fist. "Those girls are gonna pay," he declares.

I frown. *All this after I helped them with their log too?*

-6-

Tuesday

"Where's my jerky?" I blink the sleep from my eyes in the early morning light. All we'd done last night was clear off our beds and fall into them with barely a twitch all night long.

My stomach grumbles loud enough for Ethan's eyebrows (which have grown in nicely after our Zion National Park adventure) to go up. "I'm hungry too," he says.

He pulls a handful of trail mix from his backpack, which had been in the corner of the top bunk and entirely missed by the girls. The rumble in my stomach further poisons me against them.

Seriously? After I went back and helped them finish, how could they do this to us?

"Oh, no!" Ethan exclaims. He tugs at the corner of a familiar-looking plastic bag.

It's my beef jerky bag, except it's empty and slimy.

"What? Sadie took my jerky?" I whip the bag from Ethan's hand and peer into it. "Every single piece!" I scowl at the slime coating inside the bag.

My shoulders slump, knowing I'll have to wait until camp breakfast. But with all the exercise yesterday, I feel nearly woozy with hunger.

"Here," Aaron says, holding out a power bar. "I told you, those girls have got to pay for this."

I frown, but the evidence is clear: *they started it.*

"Hang on," Ethan says. "Where's my coonskin cap?" He drops to the floor, looking under each bed.

"I haven't seen it," I say, double-checking my things for it as I plow down the power bar.

Jim sticks his head in the door. "Boys, you got bigger things to deal with this week than getting back at the girls. Don't lose your focus. You came here to learn wilderness survival skills."

"Yeah," Aaron mutters under his breath, "but I'm gonna do both."

-7-

I step out of Cabin 3 and sigh. The Rocky Mountains surrounding me nearly take my breath away. "Wow!" I whisper into the perfect silence of the early morning. Sunlight cuts through the trees like bars of gold, and fog floats on the breeze.

I shiver, recalling how the thick mist at the Smoky Mountains had been so disorienting. I squat, looking at the grass heavy with dew. Trails cut through it, weaving here and there. Some are tiny—leaving only a solid trail of darker green grass with the silver coating of dew knocked off. I imagine the mouse that most likely made them, scurrying along.

Farther away I see more trails with paw prints separated by the stride of a larger creature. This outdoor sort of peace—the kind where the crisp scent of pine, the silence pierced only by the voices of birds, and the hugeness of the world combine for a perfect moment—seeps into me.

A blur of movement catches my eye. It's reddish-brown fur that appears for half a breath in the clump of trees to my right. The boys come to the door being too loud. "Shh!" I hiss at them, still crouched low, holding out my hand. Bunched up in the doorway, they freeze.

"What?" Dan whispers, scanning the trees.

Slowly, I point to the small section of fur that's still visible. I hear their gasps behind me as the creature shifts, and they catch the motion. I try to see its outline; then above where I'm looking, something darker flickers. *An ear!*

My heart pounds as the tasseled top of the creature's ear twitches again, just beyond a tree trunk. Aaron sneezes, the sound like a gunshot in the silence. I flinch at a rush of motion, and the outline of a short tail flashes for barely a moment. The creature is gone.

Caught up in the moment, Miguel whispers in awe, "It was a mountain lion!"

"No, it wasn't," I say. "Didn't you see the pointed tip of its ear?"

"Wow! A cougar!" Ethan says.

I roll my eyes. "It was a bobcat! Pointy ears, short tail."

"No, it had a long tail; I saw it," Dan insists.

How can we have such different memories of seeing the same animal?

Jim steps out of the cabin. "What's the delay? I thought you all were starving."

"We saw a cougar!" Miguel nearly shouts.

"It was a bobcat," I assert.

"No kidding? Well, I've never seen a lion around here, that's for sure. Let's get some grub; we've got a full day ahead of us."

By the time we fill our trays with breakfast food

in the main lodge, my stomach is growling. The girls push a small rolling cart from the kitchen. A big dispenser of ice-cold lemonade and cups are on it.

I nearly smile at Sadie until I remember what the girls did to our cabin. They sure seem pleased as they giggle and whisper. As the line shuffles forward, the lemonade container drains quickly. I set mine on my tray and sit down with the boys.

Aaron glares at the girls and then picks up his cup. "We can't let them get away with what they did in our cabin." He takes a big gulp, and his face immediately contorts. His free hand goes to his throat, and he spews the mouthful into the aisle.

All around the cafeteria, boys are spitting *lemonade* everywhere.

"Oh, man!" Aaron erupts. Standing up, he wipes his mouth with his sleeve. The girls explode into all-out laughter, and I sniff my cup carefully. *Pickles?* No, that odd scent is hot peppers. They must have poured pickled pepper juice into the water instead of lemon.

Jim takes a small sip and grimaces. "All right, very funny, girls. Come clean up the cafeteria and then dump all these cups in the kitchen."

Zenya taunts every boy who had gotten a mouthful as she helps clean up. I must admit, I'm more ready to give them some payback.

Sadie reaches out to take our cups. "It was *her* idea!" she defends Zenya's prank. Then she apologizes, shrugs her shoulders, and leaves abruptly.

But she still laughed—just like the others. I cross my arms. *If Sadie can dish it out, then she can take it too.*

"I told you, we've got to get them back!" We all nod at Aaron's comment.

We toss around 100 ideas by the time we're gathered in the field. I look around for Ethan; he must be in the restroom.

A wild cry splits the air…

- 8 -

Then I hear a crazed giggle. I look up to see Sadie running with her hands extended above her head. She grabs a tree branch, changing direction so fast it doesn't seem humanly possible. Then with squirrel-like speed, she shimmies up the trunk of the tree.

"This is AWESOME!"

The blood drains out of my face at that tone. "Sadie! No!" I yell, but she has already jumped from way too high in the tree. She hits the ground and starts running again.

"Zenya!" I shout, my heart pounding hard in my chest. "Did she eat sugar?"

Zenya holds up a sugar stick candy wrapper. My mouth falls open in horror. *It's empty.*

Ethan arrives at my side, "What's up? Oh, is that Sadie?" He scowls as she leaps the picnic table. He glances at me sharply. "She didn't…"

I nod. "She did."

"Oh, no!" he groans.

Together we break forward, shouting her name. I veer off toward Jim; we need lots of help if we ever hope to catch her before she hurts herself.

"JIM!" I scream, "My sister ate sugar! We've got to catch her!"

He frowns, calmly flipping through the sheets on his clipboard. "Sadie Rawlings. Oh, right. There is a note here that says she's not supposed to have sugar. It doesn't say that she's allergic…"

His head snaps up as the emergency bell tolls long and loud. Sadie is swinging from it, using her legs to gain height with every pass.

Below her, Ethan snatches at her legs, trying to catch her. She is not about to be caught. She twists lithely out of his reach. I cringe as she lets go, performing a perfect somersault in midair.

"Hey! Stop that!" Jim shouts.

My shoulders slump in relief as she lands safely. I shake Jim's forearm. "We've got to catch her; sugar makes her crazy! Dangerous!"

As if to prove my point, she snatches the lids off two metal garbage cans and takes off through the yard, clanging them together and screaming at the top of her lungs.

Leaving Jim in the dust, I rush after her, yelling, "Stop, Sadie!"

Sensing Ethan and me closing in on her, she zigs toward the nearest cabin and ramps off a picnic table, uses a signpost as a launching pad, and somehow ends up on the roof.

"Hey! Get down from there!" Jim shouts, with his hands gripping his head.

She turns toward us, sticks her thumbs in her ears, wiggles her fingers, and sticks out her tongue at us. "Catch me if you can!" she yells, and then performs several cartwheels across the roof of the cabin.

Caroline screams, running toward the scene. "What is wrong with her?"

"She ate sugar! We've got at least ten more minutes until she returns to normal. She's never had that much at once before!"

By now, nearly the entire camp is gathered, gasping in unison as Sadie launches off the roof, soaring like Supergirl. Paralyzed, Caroline screams again. But Sadie grips a tree branch, her body straight as an arrow as she flips over the branch, then lands on the ground in a perfect Olympic pose.

"Aaron, catch her!" I shout. He's the fastest kid at camp and my only hope of saving Sadie.

He takes off, but she just giggles over her shoulder and runs like the wind. As they rush around the field, she seemingly possesses superhuman speed. She rounds the corner at the far end and starts back toward us. Aaron is way behind now, his face red, gasping for air.

Jim explodes into action as she passes him, leaping into a full-body tackle. Ethan, Dan, and Miguel pile on top.

"Whew!" I wipe my brow in relief. But a wild struggle ensues, and somehow Sadie pops out from underneath them.

"Ta-da!" she shouts with her arms spread wide, grinning.

"NO!" Aaron is dragging in breath, finally catching up. Sadie leaps away from him and straight into my arms. I bear hug her as her momentum knocks us both to the ground. I feel like I am wrestling an alligator.

Finally, she goes still, and her sweet little voice reaches me. "Isaiah?"

I look down to find the crazed expression gone from her eyes.

"Isaiah? Why did you tackle me?"

I pant, "You…ate…sugar."

"Oh, yeah," she says. "It tasted so good!"

I slump back, releasing her. "Never do that again."

"Why not?" she asks, standing up and brushing herself off.

"You were doing cartwheels on the roof!"

"Really?" she asks, eyeing me.

Caroline stares at her like she might return—like she might turn back into "Sugar Sadie Supergirl" at any second. "It's true."

"Oh," Sadie says. "Did anybody happen to get it on video?"

I smack my forehead with my palm. We're parched after chasing Sadie, so Jim takes a group of us back to the cafeteria for a drink.

As we round the back of the building, Jim's voice makes us freeze. "Stop! Look right there," he whispers, pointing ahead.

- 9 -

I gasp as I catch a motion straight ahead.

"You are seeing a New Mexico meadow jumping mouse," Jim says. "They're endangered because of habitat loss. See how long its back legs and tail are compared to a common mouse like the deer mouse? These mice live in fields and at the edges of woods."

We watch the jumping mouse carefully sniff its way across the path. Faster than lightning, something to its right strikes. We all jump, but not as high as the mouse; with its back legs extended he leaps nearly as high as my hips, narrowly evading the rattlesnake's attack.

Rocky Mountain Challenge

"Whoa!" I exclaim.

Jim pushes us back with his arms. "I didn't even see the snake! That was close!"

The mouse is long gone, unharmed, and we watch in fascination as the snake recoils.

I shiver, noting its wide triangular-shaped head and the thickness of its body.

"You all run back and tell Caroline to bring the snake collection equipment. This fellow is going to have to be relocated. A kids' camp—even a survival camp—is no place for him."

A while later, back in the main field, Caroline waves her hands for silence. "All right! Listen up, today's skill to learn is shelter building. I know most of you brought hatchets, right?"

All around me, kids whoop and holler, excited to get an opportunity to use them.

"Safety always comes first. If you see someone using one, give the person at least 15 feet of space. Our challenge for today is to build survival shelters that can sustain a heavy storm—a storm also known as...*Jim*." On cue, he strikes a pose, flexing his impressive muscles.

"You may only use whatever you have on you now, and you may not go back to your cabins to get anything else. You may also use anything from the surrounding woods."

Ethan mutters as he elbows me. "We should do well then if your pockets are as full as normal."

I grin. "Oh, yeah."

Rocky Mountain Challenge

"In a true survival situation, you are often faced with the sudden arrival of a predicament—something you didn't plan. Each team's shelter will receive a score at the end of one hour. Go!"

Ideas fill my mind as 24 kids rush in different directions. The first thing we'll need is some good straight branches. I pull my small folding hatchet from the side pocket of my cargo pants and snap it open, running through my list of pocket supplies.

- ☑ One scrap of twine
- ☑ A small flashlight
- ☑ A mini-ferro rod for starting fires
- ☑ One package of dental floss (which I've found to be surprisingly strong rope but haven't flossed with even once)
- ☑ Two sticks of gum
- ☑ One survival blanket (with a hole in the center from the last time I'd used it)
- ☑ Compass

Soon, I have cut two long straight branches for

the front supports. I drag them back into the clearing, laughing to see the girls still in a huddle, just talking. *What good is that going to do? Time is ticking.* I frown as I catch sight of the rest of my cabin mates emerging from the woods with logs like mine; we pile them up.

"Looks like we're building a cabin—not a shelter," Dan says, surveying our pile of wood.

"Not if we want to win! We've only got an hour..." Ethan explains.

"Some of us should work on building, and some of us should gather materials. Then we can work faster," Dan suggests.

"I'll build," Miguel, Aaron, Dan, and I quickly say in unison.

Ethan sighs. "You all have fun figuring that out; I'm going out to find pine boughs."

Aaron insists we should build a tepee, but that will take longer than a lean-to. I'm worried it won't be as strong enough with the storm named *Jim* coming so soon.

I glance at the girls, shocked to see they already have their main supports in place, and they have already gathered all the pine boughs they'll need. To make matters worse, Sadie is weaving long vines together. She had spent much of the summer learning how to make ropes from plants.

"We're way behind," I say, remembering something my dad says about too many chiefs and not enough warriors. "I'm going to help Ethan. You three had better get this figured out quick." I feel a little annoyed to leave what feels like the most important work, but we will need supplies if we plan to finish our shelter.

I smile as I catch sight of Ethan right within the woods. He's carrying a massive pile of fresh pine boughs, which are hopelessly stuck on the surrounding trees. He groans, pulling hard. "Ouch, why do these crazy needles have to be so sharp?"

He reminds me of Chiptomunkus Rex from Zion National Park; that little guy sure could fit a lot into his cheeks.

"Ethan, wait! I'll give you a hand."

Together, we wiggle the load free and trudge into the field. It looks like Dan and Miguel have convinced Aaron to go for a lean-to. They're trying to lash the main supports together with their shoelaces, which are just too short.

"Tie them together and put them on that side. I'll take care of this end," I say, pulling out my floss.

"That will never hold!" Aaron complains.

His competitive streak must be a mile wide.

"Just trust me," I answer as I wind a few layers of the floss around the corner pieces. The dispenser is perfect at keeping it from tangling.

The hour flies by too fast. I spend the last few minutes chewing a stick of gum and smashing it into the hole in my survival blanket. Jim is counting down as we lash down the blanket on top of the boughs with more dental floss.

"Five…four…three…two…one! Hands off, teams! Your time is up!"

I back up, sweat rolling in the late summer heat.

I sure wish we had time to add a floor to give us some protection from the damp ground.

Jim drags a hose from the main lodge. *I guess the storm is going to be more serious than I had thought.* The counselors gather around the shelter that the Cabin 2 campers had constructed. So do we.

"Wow! Impressive job!" Caroline smiles wide. "I like your flag."

I see their team had scraped their number into a big piece of bark.

"Okay, Cabin 2, everybody get inside!" Jim barks. I can see he is getting happier by the minute. "Today's storm blew in from the northeast, just like the prevailing wind."

They groan as they squish next to each other in the small space. They had built their opening pointed right into the wind.

"Each shelter will be scored in three ways: by how dry the campers are after the storm, the structural integrity of the dwelling, and extra points will be given for ingenuity."

Dan screws up one side of his nose. "What's *integrity* mean?"

Ethan drapes one long arm over his shoulders. "Oh, young one, I shall teach you the meaning of this *mysterious* word." Then he wiggles his fingers and lowers his voice as if telling a secret. "It means…'to be honest and have strong moral principles, or in this case, strength.'"

"Oh," Dan says, "thanks."

"No problem. I'll give you that one for free."

"Well then, what's *ingenuity* mean?" Dan asks.

"That will cost you."

"How much?"

"The candy bar in your pocket."

Dan narrows his eyes. "How do you know what I have in my pocket?"

"Oh, trust me, I know where the candy is. It's my sixth sense that I call the *Yum Factor*."

"Okay," Dan pulls out the flattened bar.

"*Ingenuity*, sir, means 'the quality of being clever, original, or inventive.'"

"Oh, man, I think the girls will win on that one," Dan moans as Ethan slurps up the melted chocolate from the wrapper.

Jim turns on the hose and starts spraying. A chorus of shouts rises from the boys of Cabin 2 as water squirts straight through their misplaced door.

"Ha-ha!" At least the storm named *Jim* is happy.

"All right, everybody out; here comes the wind!" Jim drops the hose as the boys rush out, soaked to the skin and dripping wet. I almost wish we had copied their door so we could cool off too.

Jim's wide hands rattle the shelter; the main structure holds, but most of the boughs and leaves they piled up fall off. The next two shelters fare about the same, except one cabin had built their door pointed south like us, so they came out only partially wet from leaks.

I bite the inside of my cheek as we file into our shelter, hoping the survival blanket won't slip off during "the storm."

"We've got plenty of room in here!" Aaron says, pleased with our construction.

The water pounds the steep slope of the back wall. It's more like the sound of hail on the survival blanket. I wince as one drop hits my forehead.

"Cabin 3, come on out!" Jim says, and I sigh in relief as I scan the other boys. Dan has one wet splotch on his shoulder, and Ethan's knee is damp from kneeling on the ground. We're almost completely dry!

"Is this...dental floss?" Jim asks.

"Yes, sir."

Jim's impressed look turns into a grin as every single piece of our shelter holds together!

"Guess the floss was a great idea!" Aaron's flying high, pumped that we had done so well.

We all herd over to the girls' shelter. Smiling, Zenya swings open a sturdy little door that moves nicely on hinges made of...bracelets! They shut the door behind them and giggling echoes from inside. Jim turns on the hose, and the water rebounds off the wide strips of bark they had wisely chosen to use as shingles.

I had seen that dead log, even climbed over it once, but I hadn't once thought of using its loose bark. The water shuts off, and a tiny hatch at the top flips up. Their giggling gets louder through the small opening, then a thick white powder that looks a lot like smoke rises through the hole. But it smells suspiciously like baby powder. With their fake fire, my hopes of winning sink.

"Wow!" Jim says, clearly impressed.

Ethan frowns. "And that shelter, my friends, shows *ingenuity*."

Aaron drives his fist into his thigh.

We break for lunch, crowding around the cabin score sheets after Jim adds this morning's marks.

"Oh, no!" Aaron's cry is no surprise. The girls have slipped ahead of us with a ton of extra points for their door and smoke. "We'll get them this afternoon," he declares.

I'm not so sure. Cabin 2 isn't that far behind us.

This time for lunch, we get real lemonade from Frankie, the cook. I press the cold cup against my cheek.

Excitement ripples through the cafeteria as the counselors talk about the next event. *A zip line! This sport is something I've always wanted to do!*

- 10 -

My breath comes faster as we hike up to the highest point at Camp Wilderness.

"Wow!" The view from the wooden zip-line tower is breathtaking. We all grow quiet.

"That's Rocky Mountain National Park. Our camp borders it on two sides. Tomorrow we're heading into the park for some waterfall rappelling at Chasm Falls, plus you'll each get a chance to become Junior Rangers," Caroline says.

"Yes!" Sadie, Ethan, and I say at the same time. For a second, it seems like old times when the three of us were inseparable. I push off the twinge. I sure can't wait to add my fourth Ranger badge to my trusty backpack the bear had shredded at Great Smoky Mountains National Park.

Caroline gives instructions for getting into the safety harnesses and carefully checks that we've all got them on snugly.

"Everyone, now listen up! We've got nearly a mile of zip line ahead. Jim is waiting at the far end, and he'll guide you to a stop. During your zip, you can slow down by using *only* your right hand—the one with the leather glove."

I clench my right fist tightly. *The leather feels super tough.*

"**Never**, I repeat, **never** grab the main cable in front of you. The slider will pinch your hand, and you will get stuck out on the line. If you want to slow down, grab the cable behind the slider and gently increase the pressure. Who's first?"

Hands shoot up all around, and I survey the mountains as we wait. When the first boy attaches his trolley and steps off the platform, I am unprepared for the unique, high-pitched, laser-like whine of the trolley on the cable. The sound causes a shiver to run down my spine.

Caroline's radio crackles with Jim's voice. "Clear for the next rider."

Zenya is trying to back down the tight set of steps to the takeoff platform, but the press of kids prevents her.

"Ugh...I don't..." Zenya mutters. One foot is on the top platform, and her face has a strange green tint to it. The boy ahead of her hollers long and loud as he steps into thin air, then is away, high above the treetops.

Zenya shudders. "No!" She giggles, sounding embarrassed. "Ah, no. I can't do this." Her words come out too fast—all jumbled together.

"Sure, you can," Caroline encourages her. "Once you're going, it's a blast! I promise you'll feel like you're flying!"

"Yeah, that's the problem. I don't want to fly."

Aaron laughs and smirks, "She's nothing but a chicken!" I frown as hurt flashes across Zenya's face.

"What's the point of hating your sister so much?" I ask.

He shrugs. "She's my sister." He responds like I'm dumb for asking.

"That's exactly why you shouldn't," I mutter.

The other girls encourage Zenya, but thir support only makes her more resistant to the idea.

She grabs her stomach. "Ooh…I think I'm going to…you know."

Her green tinge is strong enough that I back up to get out of range. Caroline radios one of the other counselors, and Zenya hurries down the platform farther from the treetops and the clear, blue sky.

Sadie goes next. She steps off the platform with absolutely no hesitation. Her loud *"Wahooooo!"* echoes down the valley. Her excitement makes my feet itch to leave the ground.

Finally, it's my turn. With my toes perched on the edge of the platform, I take a deep breath. The leaves shimmer in the light breeze below me. Eventually, I remember to let out a breath of air.

"You're all set, Isaiah."

I nod, knowing my mouth is too dry to respond. I grip the rope that connects my harness to the cable and lean forward.

"WHOA!" Gravity takes over, and for a second, I free-fall with my legs kicking. Then the cable takes my weight.

Zzzzziiippp! I'm flying! I pick up speed until tears squeeze from my eyes. As I descend, I drop below the tree line, now rushing through the narrow alley cut through the woods.

A hawk swoops low, feathers glinting golden in the sun as he studies me with one eye. I feel like I receive something distinctive from his fearless heart. He tilts one wing in what seems like a salute, lifting suddenly out of sight. I fly over the stream, refreshed by the cool current of air above the water.

"Brakes, Isaiah! Brakes!" Jim shouts, making me flinch.

"Wh…what?" Reality hits quickly, and I nearly reach for the cable ahead of me.

"Behind you!" Jim shouts and nods in relief as I grasp the line correctly. The glove heats up fast, but I slow as I near the ground. Jim reaches out and helps me find my footing.

"How was your flight?" he asks.

"AWESOME!" My voice comes out way too loud, but I don't care. For a moment, I was free! *Weightless!*

- 11 -

In the dark of night, we are the shadows. Silently, we cut toward the girls' cabin, and soon we've accomplished mission one: sneaking into the deserted girls' restroom. We open the water tanks on the back of each toilet and pour in the contents of three glow sticks each. One flush produces an incredibly eerie glow on the inside of each toilet. We slip through the darkness to the girls' cabin and press our backs against the rough wood.

Aaron has a bowl of melted marshmallows and a short stick in his hands; Ethan is holding a jar of chocolate sprinkles. While Dan, Miguel, and I keep watch, both slip inside, their faces painted in camouflage. From where I'm stationed, I can barely make out Aaron as he carefully paints melted marshmallows on the girls' shoelaces. By morning, the hardened marshmallows will turn into something like concrete, making them impossible to untie. I release a breath as they emerge, and we sneak back across the distance to our cabin.

"Shh! Freeze!" Ethan's harsh whisper makes us all drop into the embrace of cold, dewy grass. Still as stone, we watch a beam of a flashlight sweep beyond us. Three of the girls whisper as they make for the restrooms.

"This is gonna be awesome!" Aaron can barely contain himself. As the restroom door slams shut, I hold my breath and count. *One…two…three…*

"*Eeh-haa!*" Three screams meld into one as the girls explode to the door. The flashlight bounces crazily as they run toward their cabin. A part of me is glad Sadie isn't among them, but then I remember her laughter with the pickled pepper juice.

We can hardly hold back our wild laughter.

Voices echo from the girls' cabin. "What's all over my pillow?"

"It's mouse poo!" Another set of screams sends us over the edge. *Ethan's chocolate sprinkles had worked exactly as planned.*

"Come on! Let's get out of here!" Ethan leads us back to Cabin 3. I notice the bandanna he has tied around his head. *Sure makes him look tough.*

All three pranks had been his ideas, and I must admit I've never seen this side of Ethan. I crawl into my bed, jerking up when my pillow crinkles loudly in my ear. *What in the world...*

Dan clicks on a flashlight, pulling a plastic bag from inside his pillowcase. "The girls!"

"Ha! What a lame prank!" Aaron mocks. "What were we supposed to do? Scream?" He pulls the plastic from his pillow and lets it float to the floor. With my pillow back to normal, I settle into the comfort of my sleeping bag. In the dark, Ethan's voice sums up our thoughts: "This means war!"

- 12 -

Wednesday

I stretch as morning's light intrudes.

"Come on, Cabin 3! Rise and shine." *Jim's voice is entirely too happy for this early in the morning.*

"Ugh." My muscles are feeling the effort from the first couple days of camp. Ethan wiggles out of his sleeping bag, and Jim bursts out laughing.

I snap awake and look at Ethan. "Why are you… shimmering?" I blink at him. *This must be a dream.*

Jim clamps a hand over his mouth, trying to keep from laughing, but he can't quite make it. "FFF…Funny…Ha-ha!"

Ethan's skin and clothes are coated in a thick

layer of green glitter. The air all around him is shimmering as well because he's shedding so much of the glitter.

Dan rolls out of his bed, and Ethan's eyes go wide, staring straight at him. Dan is just as glittery, but he is blue.

"What?" He looks down at himself in horror.

Jim doubles over laughing.

I wiggle my toes, feeling something sandy. "Oh, no!"

As I had fallen asleep last night, I wondered how I had gotten so much sand in my sleeping bag. Slowly, I pull out my arm. *I'm as silver as a fish!*

Aaron's voice cracks as he leaps from his bed; his dark skin is now bright red!

Jim can hardly speak. He's laughing so hard, "Co…co…come on, Miguel. Let's see what color you are!"

Miguel sighs. "I'm gold," he says flatly. "It's all over my pillow." He turns his head; one cheek is plastered with gold glitter.

"One thing is clear…the girls are more intelligent and sneaky than you gave them credit for," Jim notes.

"We are going to have to up our game," Ethan declares.

We stride to the showers, leaving trails of glitter through the grass. It doesn't matter how much I scrub; there's no way all that glitter will come off. What's worse is there's no way to get it out of my sleeping bag—not by a long shot. We had beaten them on the cabin railings as hard as we could, but clearly, we are going to wake up shimmering every single morning.

By the time we assemble in the main field, we bear the heavy burden of mocking from the boys in the other cabins. Ethan is immediately dubbed *Shamrock*, and Dan is named the *Smurf*.

"Those girls are going to pay dearly for their pranks!" Ethan promises.

Jim checks his watch, looking toward the girls' cabin.

"Umm...they are going to be late, sir," Aaron says through clenched teeth.

Finally, the girls filter in, most of them holding their shoes, working at the stubborn laces. Sadie is wearing one shoe, but she is struggling with the laces on the other.

I must admit; they had outdone us by far. *What's fake mouse poo, glowing toilets, and sticky shoes compared to the burning shame of being glittered?*

During breakfast, Jim gives directions for the day. "We are heading into the Rocky Mountain National Park. We expect each of you to be at the top of your wilderness skills today." He reads off a list of park rules that I'm already familiar with. "How many of you already have earned a Junior Ranger badge?" Only two hands other than Ethan's, Sadie's, and mine go up.

"Okay, by the end of today, you should all have at least one. So, who is ready to rappel down a waterfall?"

We all shout, then race to the bus waiting to take

us to the park. It's less than a five-minute drive to the huge entrance sign.

"All right, campers, it's time for our traditional survival week picture. Everybody, gather in front of the sign. We'll send one of these pictures home with each of you."

Unbelievable! I shake my head as I step off the bus, my silver arms shimmering in the bright light. Every single time I pose in front of a national park sign, I look ridiculous. I scowl hard at the camera. *There's no point in pretending that being glittered like this is okay.*

Still hanging my head, I climb back onto the bus, but I can't resist the wildness of the park. Adventure is waiting just ahead; and shimmery or not, I know today is going to be a wonderful day. The bus travels about two miles into the park, and I smash my cheek against the window to see the road sign as we turn—Endovalley Road.

We pass the Endovalley picnic area and turn onto the one-way Old Fall River Road. The tires are louder on the rough seasonal road. Then we pull up next to the Chasm Falls Trailhead.

"Listen up, campers!" Jim claps his hands at the front of the bus. "Camp Wilderness is the only one ever to rappel these falls. This experience is a once-in-a-lifetime one!" He makes a loud woofing sound in a deep voice, pumping his hands into the air and building excitement for everyone.

We copy him until the windows rattle with the sound. "Okay, okay, pay attention. Since you are the only people on the planet who get to do this, you're going to do exactly what we tell you to do, right?"

"Yes, sir!" we chorus in reply.

"The water of the Fall River only reaches a balmy temperature of 70° in August every year. Good thing for you, that's right now. Most of the time the water is a deadly 37°. This activity is ***never*** to be repeated on your own at these falls. You got that? Understand, right?"

We nearly run over Jim as we rush off the bus.

C. R. Fulton

Caroline leads the way toward the trailhead. I read a posted sign with the following warning:

> *Danger: swift water! Stay back from the river and the riverbanks. Boulders are treacherously slick! If you fall in, the icy water will quickly incapacitate you, and the swift currents can kill you.*

Well, isn't that message encouraging?

- 13 -

I stop at a wooden box and pull out a park map. Sadie slides up next to me and does the same. We have both learned how important it is to carry a map in our pocket and in our mind.

Her eyes flick up to mine. "Nice skin," she says, with no meanness in her voice.

"Nice shoelaces," I respond easily. We both look down at her shoes with the laces completely stiff, and my legs still shiny despite my best efforts.

She giggles. "I thought I'd never get them on!"

That comment makes me laugh—just like she always manages to do. I feel like old times when we weren't just siblings, but friends. Then she replaces her map in the wooden box, and I walk over to the Cabin 3 boys, and she to the girls. Suddenly, we're adversaries again. That thought doesn't settle well in my stomach.

The path to Chasm Falls is rough and formed from huge boulders. Navigating the trail takes all my concentration to get to the bottom. Soon the deep voice of the falls is rattling in my chest, and a ranger directs us through a wooden stockade fence that keeps most park visitors away from the falls. Caroline motions us up toward Jim, who's pulling a thick coil of rope from his shoulder.

"Can I give you a hand?" I ask.

Jim points to a large oak tree. "We aren't allowed to set any climbing bolts into the rocks here, so we tie off to this old tree." Handing me the rope, I walk the end around, noting the moss growing on one side of the thick tree. That's the north side because moss only grows on bark that gets the least sun.

"We're going to use a running bowline knot. Do you know what that is?"

"No, sir," I say as Ethan walks up.

"Well, it all has to do with a rabbit's coming out of his hole."

"Oh, I see! So, we shoot the rabbit?" Ethan asks.

"Maybe *knot*. Ha-ha. *Get it, knot?*" Jim takes the length of the rope and drops it over Ethan's shoulders. Then he makes a loop of the end with his left hand. "The rabbit comes out of the hole." He pokes the tail end of the rope through his loop. "He goes around the back of the tree, and then back into his hole."

He takes the rope off Ethan's shoulders and pulls it tight around the tree. Next, he flings the length out over the falls, and I watch it uncoil as it seems to drop forever. "Now we're ready to suit up."

For all 24 campers plus Jim to get into their safety harnesses and tighten down their helmets takes a while. Dan hitches his harness belt even tighter. "Do you think Zenya will fail this one too? The score between the girls, us, and Cabin 2 is way too close."

Aaron looks over at the four pink helmets

against all our blue ones. "Not a chance! She can do this sort of thing. Don't worry though...we got everybody here beat! We're Cabin 3, and we'll bring them to their knees!"

We all gather close to the drop-off, which looks a lot higher than it did from the viewing area. From here, a fine mist is rising from the falls; it cools my skin as the updraft of air ruffles my hair.

"Well, Isaiah, I'm going down first to assess our knot. Let's hope Ethan didn't shoot the rabbit. You'll come down next."

I nod at Jim.

Caroline explains the basics of rappelling, how our weight and the friction brake on the rope work together to create a smooth descent. Jim backs over the big round boulder at the top of the falls and whoops loudly as he drops over the edge, using his legs to navigate the steep, slippery walls of rock and water.

Soon, I'm leaning back on the rope with one hand behind me, trying to figure out how to control my speed. I crab-walk awkwardly down the first sheer rock. Then my hands, legs, weight, and the equipment all start to work together so that now I feel like a spider dropping easily along its web.

The cool water makes me shiver, but the power of the falls fills me with wonder. In the wilderness, its thunder drowns out everything else. Filled with the freshest scent I've ever smelled, the air tingles. I look up; the trees so high above me reach for the sky, and the hot sun kisses my face. I find I can choose a path, either through the pounding water or right beside it.

I slide my fingers into the brilliant water, and inside I'm changed—bigger somehow, more confident for having this experience. I'm completely soaked and grinning from ear to ear when I reach Jim at the bottom.

He high fives me. "Nice descent, man!"

- 14 -

The badge on the cover of my Rocky Mountain National Park Junior Ranger booklet displays a bighorn ram, which reminds me of our Zion adventure. Sadie had saved the life of a bighorn, and at a crucial time, the ram had returned the favor.

I bite my lip, wishing momentarily that all the pranking and competition had never started.

I look up to see Aaron and Dan comparing their finished pages. We're in Hidden Valley, a specific area reserved for future Junior Rangers located near the east end of Rocky Mountain National Park.

"All right, campers, we've got a full schedule for today," Jim announces. "It's mapping and signaling day. Everybody, get to studying and finish your Junior Ranger booklets so far."

"It's weird to just sit down and finish an entire Junior Ranger journey at one time," Ethan says as he settles next to me.

"Yeah, it feels more like school."

Really, that's okay with me. My body is glad for the rest. Rappelling had taken more energy than I had thought it would. I fill in a few pages, glad to know most of the answers already. A bighorn is pictured on the "Alpine Tundra" page as well. I chew the inside of my cheek as memories of Zion come back even stronger—especially remembering the way my heart had sunk to my toes when the thief held Sadie in his cruel hands.

I look over at her now. She's sitting by herself, tapping her pen on her chin as she reads. She's the best sister ever—*my family*—and that relationship is forever. She glances up at me and smiles. She had been so brave while rappelling, and I'm proud of her.

A sudden motion catches my eye. Aaron is pitching pebbles at Zenya. She whips around, scowling at him. He laughs, then throws another. Zenya gets up and moves over beside Sadie.

I sigh, studying the picture again. Aaron and Zenya are more like two rams slamming their heads together; and the truth is, their behavior has infected both Sadie and me. Deep down I hate the separation between us. It's better when we treat each other with respect.

I sigh, filling in the page. I don't know how to change that separation—not with the pranks and payback raging so thick between our cabins.

Aaron comes over to join Ethan and me. He turns to the page labeled "Food Web."

"See, we boys are right here at the top of the food chain—just like this cougar." He taps the paper with one long finger.

"Yeah…" Ethan adds, "just like the one we've been seeing at camp. That's me, the lone ruler of the land." Flexing his arm to show strength, he forms a slightly less-than-impressive bicep, but I keep that thought to myself.

"It was a bobcat," I say flatly.

"Oh, come on! It was the king of the beasts—just like me," Ethan insists.

"Well, what's the point exactly? I mean, why do we have to prove that we're better than anybody else? My dad says we should judge everything by the fruit that it makes. Right now, there's no good fruit coming from all the pranking, just a bunch of thorns scratching everybody—even you, King Shamrock."

My not-so-subtle reminder makes Ethan hang his head, but only for a second. "I got the perfect idea to get them back for the glitter bombs."

I throw up my hands in amazement. "See? You can't even hear me. Why don't we call a truce and start concentrating on why we came here in the first place? We came to learn how to survive the wilderness—not each other!"

"You do realize the glitter will never come out

of our sleeping bags? It's not something I can just let go of," Aaron declares.

The other boys gather around as Ethan outlines his new plan. They keep adding to Ethan's prank until my stomach is in a knot. *They're not thinking straight; somebody could get hurt during this one.*

But I cannot convince them of the foolishness of this prank no matter how hard I try. By the time we're taking our Junior Ranger pledge, I'm teetering between telling Jim about their plan or sabotaging it myself.

I finger my fourth National Park Junior Ranger badge, wondering what to do about the prank. *I've just made a commitment to protect everything wild, but what about my sister?*

- 15 -

The smell of campfire smoke clings to us as we crawl into our bunks. My body is worn out, but my heart is so full. I had enjoyed an amazing day. A soft scratching sound catches my ear; then there's a knock on the door. Ethan strides over to open it, but right before he reaches the knob, an explosion of white fluff coats him from head to toe.

I'm out of bed in a second, rushing toward him, slipping on the slick white foam. Giggles and swift footsteps give away the culprits on the other side of the door.

Ethan is stiff as a board, with only his huge blue eyes showing through the thick coating of shaving cream. "Those girls aren't gonna get away with that!" he exclaims.

Dan wrenches open the door and picks up a limp sandwich bag. "Here's how they did it. They filled the bag, then stuffed the seal under the door. When they heard you get close, one of them stomped on the bag."

"I know which one it was too," Aaron says with fire in his eyes.

"Zenya," Ethan growls, wiping his face. Soon, we're sneaking across the dark yard outside our cabin. Up ahead, Ethan has a short piece of rope. After the boys set up the rest of the prank, he needs to slip into the girls' cabin, throw the rope onto Zenya's sleeping bag and shout *"Snake!"* The plan is for all the girls to run out of the cabin where the rest of the boys will be waiting.

My problem is, I could never forgive myself if or when somebody gets hurt—not with what they've planned. Sweat beads up on my upper lip, and I wipe my slick palms on my jeans. I should have told Jim. *What was I thinking? If they wouldn't listen to me before, why would they now?*

We freeze as a low growl rumbles in the night.

"Was that a bear?" Aaron's voice barely squeaks in my ear.

"No," I whisper, the rest of my words cut off as the growl comes again. The hair on my arms stands on end as the growl rises in pitch to a snarl.

The boys huddle closer together. I see movement in the brush ahead. Someone is gripping my arm, fingernails biting into my skin.

"It's the lion!" Ethan's voice trembles in the pitch dark.

I remind myself it's just a bobcat; but in the dark, where teeth and claws rule, I'm not so sure. A thought occurs to me. "It's between us and the girls' cabin," I whisper.

Another branch snaps, and everyone flinches.

"Umm…mmm…maybe we should go back." Dan takes a wobbly step backward.

"Lions are territorial." I add to their fear, hope

bursting forth that they might not be able to execute the prank. At some unseen signal, we rush back to Cabin 3. I barely keep up, and as I reach the steps, I whisper over my shoulder, "Thank you."

That cat has no idea what kind of disaster it just averted.

- 16 -

Thursday

"Is this edible wood sorrel or poisonous clover?" Caroline asks Sadie. She and Jim are evaluating all the campers on what we've learned about finding food in the wild.

Sadie picks up the clover-shaped leaves and inspects the stem carefully. "It's wood sorrel because it has a line of hair running up one side of its stem."

"Correct!" Caroline smiles at her.

Sadie stuffs it into her mouth, making a face at its strong lemon-like flavor.

"The good thing is wood sorrel is sugar-free!"

Sadie's face grows pink at Caroline's joke.

Next in line is Ethan, who steps up. Jim says, "Is this a wild blueberry or poisonous pokeweed?"

Ethan frowns at the sprig of deep purplish berries. "Edible!" he says easily after looking at it for only half a second.

Jim makes a loud buzzer sound. "Wrong! You've just eaten pokeweed, and you might toss your cookies. Or worse, depending on how many you ate, you could die!"

Even though Ethan hasn't touched them, he falls to the ground, clutching his stomach and groaning. "Not my cookies!"

Everyone laughs; then a bunch of boys put on a show of mourning Ethan as he rolls around on the ground.

"What will we do without Ethan?" Dan cries, falling dramatically to his knees.

Ethan's eyes snap open as he pulls a rope candy from his back pocket and stuffs it in his mouth. "All better now!" He hops up and heads toward the back of the line.

"Remember, foraging for wild food is no joke when it's just you and the forest. Next!" Jim says.

It's my turn now, and I chew my lower lip as Caroline pulls a brown root from her bin. It's got one sprig of green sticking out the top.

"Please identify this root and tell me if it's edible."

I take it and roll it in my hands. "Well, it's got thin layers of skin and…" I poke my fingernail into the stem and then sniff. "Whew! It sure smells strong. The green part is round, not flat like a stem…so it's a wild onion. Edible."

"Excellent!"

"Um. Do I *have* to eat it?" The strong odor is still burning my nose.

Caroline laughs. "No, but if you were hungry, you might be surprised by all the things you would eat to stay alive."

Finding and sanitizing water is the next activity. I think I'll get extra points for making a filter from my shirt and half of a water bottle. I scoop my water carefully from the very top of the stream, not dipping near the bottom where silt will ruin it.

My water is nearly clear, and by the time I filter it through pebbles, moss, and sand in the other half of the bottle, it's ready to boil.

Next, we each receive a clear plastic bag, and Jim instructs us to find a low-hanging branch with broad leaves. Then we carefully force the bag over the branch and leaves and tie it tight to the stem.

"Now, make sure the pointed corner of your bag is near the bottom so the water will collect there," Jim explains.

"What water?" Ethan asks, staring at his leaf bag that is perfectly dry on the inside.

"You'll see by tonight. Who is ready to go river rafting?"

Every single camper erupts with excitement. Jim waves his hands for silence. "I'll take that response as a yes. Everybody needs to bring his or her helmet from yesterday. You've got ten minutes to get ready. We are heading back into Rocky Mountain

National Park, and we'll end up right back here where the Fall River runs past the campground."

"Yes!" I leap high, one fist in the air, and then I run for my blue helmet. I climb the wide stairs of the bus and squeeze in next to Aaron and Ethan. They've got their heads together, whispering.

"Isaiah, wait until you hear what we've got planned for tonight!" Ethan says.

"You do remember Sadie is going to suffer from your plans, right? *My sister Sadie,*" I add.

"You do remember that she snuck in and stole all your beef jerky and probably my coonskin cap too?" Ethan says, blinking rapidly.

I frown at him but don't reply. *He's right, but this pranking just doesn't sit well with me.* To be honest, I'm not sure who did what, but I can't prove anything for sure.

"Lord," I pray under my breath. "I sure could use Your help to sort this all out. I don't want anybody to get hurt."

- 17 -

As we drive past the Rocky Mountain National Park sign, that incredible feeling of freedom settles over me. I am in one of the wildest places on earth, and for right now, all I have to do is experience it.

"We will raft the Fall River—the same water that runs over Chasm Falls. We're well below that place now, and the water is fairly calm all the way to camp. Pay attention, follow the rules, and keep your eyes open! We almost always see an abundance of wildlife on this trip."

We unload at the same trailhead as before; but this time, Jim leads us down what looks like a deer path right behind the bus. This path proves even steeper than the Chasm Falls Trail, and we spread out to negotiate it safely. We end up on a wide shoal of rocks with the sparkling water of Fall River straight ahead and the towering Rockies all around us.

The mountain faces are mostly rock with only a few scraggly trees clinging here and there. Jim hauls inflatable rafts to the shore. "Wow! The river is higher than I've ever seen it. Cabin 2, load up!" he says, holding the large rubber raft still as the boys and their counselor nearly flip it.

"Easy now, you've got to treat her gently if you want to stay afloat." Jim pushes them out into deeper water, and they must paddle against the current to wait for the rest of us.

We're the last group to get in our raft, and my fingers are itching to hold an oar. Finally, everyone is on the water, and I dig my oar deep into the swirling river. The heavy resistance of the water brings a smile; I enjoy fighting against it. Ethan and I are sitting across from each other, and we fall into an easy rhythm and cadence that propels our raft to the front of the group.

The first thing I notice is the silence. Gliding over the water, I hear only the quiet plunk of drips falling from our oars when we stroke. I think all of us are feeling the majesty of this place where we're just little specks floating along in a big world.

I duck as a whoosh of wind rips through the air right above my head. "Whoa!" My shout reverberates down the canyon as a bald eagle plunges toward the water ahead, diving at full speed. Icy water sprays us as the eagle's wings beat the air, rising again while holding a slippery, wriggling fish in its talons.

Without thinking, Aaron stands up, pointing wildly at the bird. Ethan leans far to the left to see around him, and the raft tilts. Aaron's arms cartwheel, making the raft shift even further.

"Sit down!" Jim commands, half a heartbeat before my side of the raft connects with a round boulder barely hidden beneath the current.

I only get out a partial shout before I'm catapulted over Ethan and hit the water headfirst, my life vest barely slowing me down. The raft flops on top of us, and everything is dark and crazy. I come up, struggling for a breath in the air pocket beneath the raft.

"That went pretty well," Ethan says, sputtering as he treads water. Jim's head breaks the surface. "1, 2, 3, 4... Where is Miguel?"

I turn in the water; Jim is right! I don't see him anywhere. With a desperate motion, Jim kicks hard, and his strong arms flip the raft off us. I release a breath when I see Miguel swimming toward the raft and us.

"Did you..." A gush of the river makes him pause to shut his mouth. "...see that eagle?"

We take a while to scramble back into the boat, dripping, exhilarated, and floating on in search of adventure. By now we're far behind the other four boats, and we slow even more to navigate around a sandbar. We stroke hard to catch up, but Aaron and Dan can't seem to hold a steady pace. We keep bumping into opposite sides of the riverbank.

    Excited voices up ahead echo as the others pass around a bend. Jim paddles for real instead of letting us bumble around. That feeling—the one that's never failed to warn me when danger is near—shrieks across my chest. I grip the oar, digging hard in rhythm with Jim and Ethan. The raft surges forward as a scream reverberates off the rocks ahead.

    "Go!" I shout, willing Aaron and Dan to straighten up. My stomach tightens into a hard knot. *Something is wrong.*

- 18 -

The canyon ahead is still ringing with shouts. Finally, our raft noses around the bend and straight into a wall of crazy white water.

"Hold on!" Jim shouts as we're swept into a narrow chasm the wide river is trying to fit through. I grip the rope on the side of the raft as it bucks hard, launching over a rim of frothing water.

"Left! Left!" Jim screams at us, and the terror in his voice kicks me into action. I shove my oar into a sharp corner of stone that is aiming to deflate our raft. I roar as our momentum pushes me hard.

"Hold on, Isaiah! We've got to get around these rocks!"

Jim scrambles forward to help me, his powerful arms forcing the boat away from the deadly rocks. We spin crazily, the water sucking us faster and faster. A glance up ahead reveals the other boats struggling in the middle of the rapids.

"There must have been an avalanche! The river's always been wide here! Boys, stroke hard to the right!" Jim shouts. The massive pile of rock he's pointing at is straight ahead and coming up fast. My oar bites deep into the water, but it feels like sludge as we watch disaster approach.

"Eh!" Aaron drops his oar, clutching his leg as the raft slides over a submerged rock.

"Aaron, get in the center!" Jim crawls to Aaron's place and jams his oar into the rock pile so hard the end splinters. Still, the concussion has forced us into the safety of the deeper current. Aaron is still gripping his leg in the middle of the raft, so Jim grabs the boy's discarded oar.

My chest tingles from shoulder to shoulder, and I glance around wildly. A bloodcurdling scream takes my breath away. Up ahead, the girls' raft looks like a ping-pong ball as it bounces off a nasty set of rapids.

"NO!" But my voice can't stop Sadie's light form from launching into the air at the next impact! She flails as the raft rushes forward; but by the time she falls, only surging whitewater waits to swallow her. I hear someone screaming like mad, and realize it might be me. "Sadie!"

It seems like days pass before her pink helmet breaks the surface. Jim paddles wildly as the same set of rapids sucks us in. Sadie's hand rises weakly above the water. As the current draws us even closer, I tense.

"Everybody, hold on!" Jim commands.

I let go of the raft altogether, my hands spread wide. Time slows down, every movement grows distinct, and the water beads shimmer like diamonds in the brilliant light.

"Now!" I whisper to myself as I launch into the gaping maw of the river. The water seems colder, and time snaps back to its frantic pace as I search deeper and deeper for my sister.

Something soft! I grip it hard and kick like wild for the boiling surface. I gasp long and loud, pulling Sadie against my chest; the thickness of our life vests makes it difficult for me to hold on to her. She barely gets a breath before another wave takes us captive. I stroke hard with one arm and try to avoid the slicing edges of rocks.

The water heaves us up and sucks us under. It's taking everything I have to hold on to her. My lungs are burning—long since out of air. *Please, God* is all I can think as we tumble over a low falls. My feet hit the rocky bottom, and I push up desperately. We burst through the surface, and the inflatable rafts are long gone. Sadie groans in my arms. *I must get to shore!*

Just when I'm sure we're going under again, a swift current shoves us to the left. I lean hard to stay in the twisting strip of smoother water. I kick up loose pebbles, then scramble wildly onto a bank. We flop onto the gritty sand and stare at the sky. I take a few deep breaths before my muscles respond.

"Sadie…are you all right?" I lean over her and see a big gash on her bright pink helmet. I unhook the chinstrap and ease it off. Relief floods me when I don't find any blood.

"Isaiah? Where are we?" She sits up, holding her head.

"You fell in the Fall River."

"Very funny."

"No, seriously, you did."

She scowls, blinking fast. "Oh, now I remember! The rapids came up so fast!"

I look up at the far side of the canyon. "It looks like half the mountain let loose and tumbled into Fall River too."

"Must be a popular activity around here," she says with a hint of a smile.

I pull her into a tight hug. "I'm so glad you're safe. Are you hurt anywhere?"

She wiggles her fingers and toes. "Nothing major—just bruised a bit. That was one wild ride. I sure hope the others made it okay."

The wilderness seems to go on forever. There might not be another human for miles. "One thing's for sure, the river has taken them far away and here we are again—just the two of us."

- 19 -

A huge smile breaks across Sadie's face. "I've actually missed that."

"Me too." Shifting, I stand up. "Ouch. Oh. Eh." My legs had smashed into more rocks than I thought, and the adrenaline rush kept me from feeling it till now.

Sadie stands up too. "Ugh. Ow!" A giggle bubbles up. "We sound ridiculous!"

I take a step forward, but my muscles punish me for it. "Ah!"

"Ouch!"

"Ow!" I force my cramped leg muscles to stretch. We wander down the shore, groaning in pain.

"Since the river goes straight through camp, I guess the best thing to do is just follow it. It could take hours for rescue crews to find us," Sadie says, studying the steep mountains.

"Normally, staying put would be best, but this time you're right. This river is better than a highway; it will lead us straight to our goal, so let's go."

We pick our way downstream. A jumble of logs has piled up at the bend, and navigating around it takes a while. Moving gets easier as we work out most of the kinks. We walk in silence until I can't contain the question any longer. "Sadie, why did you girls ransack our cabin? Why would you take my deer jerky? Plus, Ethan's coonskin cap? Those things weren't yours." The words come out bitter.

She huffs with a hurt voice. "What? I didn't take your things. We never touched your cabin on Monday. But I could ask you the same question. That first night, it looked like a bomb went off in our cabin." Sadie's crosses her arms and tilts her head to one side like Zenya.

Absorbing this information takes a minute, and I believe her! She's as honest as the day is long. *That means we boys had assumed wrong—really wrong.* "Well, if you didn't do it, then who did?"

We stare at each other for a minute. "Was it Cabin 1 or Cabin 5? Wait, didn't you boys make all that noise in our ceiling?" Sadie asks, frowning.

"Nope, wasn't us," I say.

Her eyes widen. "Oh, we figured it was you, which makes it even scarier."

I bite my lip and think about the situation. "I haven't heard about anyone else playing pranks, have you?"

"No."

"Then it doesn't make sense that they would pull such a big prank right off and then quit entirely, does it?"

"It makes more sense than nobody doing it."

"Still, something's not right! Besides, who would steal a bag of meat and a coonskin cap? I figured you'd be the only one to notice those things."

She shakes her head. "I promise! I knew nothing of it. Besides, am I not the one who usually gives you the things you like?"

Her elbow pokes my rib, and I roll my eyes. "You're right. Sorry I jumped to conclusions. You're the best sister ever."

"You've got that right!" she says with a twinkle in her eye. "And thanks for saving me! I don't think I would've made it out of the river without you."

"Anytime," I say lightly, as if we hadn't both been in death's grip. "Truce?"

"Yeah. I hated being at odds with you, Isaiah."

"Can you imagine hating each other the way Aaron and Zenya do?" I question.

"No, that would be such an awful way to live! Every minute would be full of fighting and arguing—even inside our own house." She shivers. "Yeah. I'm so glad Mom and Dad don't let us fight. Oh, look, that's wood sorrel."

We veer off into the woods a bit and gather up handfuls of green leaves. They taste a lot like sour candy, and we enjoy munching them as we walk. My face puckers up on my second bite. "What do you figure? Three miles to Camp Wilderness?"

"Yeah, at least," she says. "I bet we'll both have blisters from our soaked shoes."

Water squishes with every step we take, making three miles seem so much longer. There isn't so much as an electric wire or ATV trail the entire way and walking along the riverbank is difficult.

I toss a stem at Sadie, and it sticks in her hair. She rolls her eyes, throws one back and trudges on. I tell myself, "That's the last time I'll ever get caught up in something that pulls my family apart. Family closeness is something deeper than any other relationship and deserves my protection."

"Have you noticed how all the boys think Ethan is the best thing since sliced bread?" I ask.

She laughs. "If only they knew he lost a war with a chipmunk!"

Now, everything seems exactly right—as if the river had reset everything inside. Now I can see clearly again. We climb over so many log jams and fallen trees that I lose count.

"Camp should come up anytime now, shouldn't it?" Sadie asks, slapping at a fly.

I scan the area. "Look! There's smoke! That must be camp there."

We push forward, cutting through the underbrush away from the river. Now I can smell the smoke, and my stomach growls. The brush ends abruptly, and we're in a small clearing with a well-tended campfire in the center. A small one-man tent sits in the shelter of some large pine trees.

"Um… Isaiah," Sadie whispers, "This isn't Camp Wilderness."

-20-

I spot a laptop sitting open on a stump in the center of the camp. Sadie's tense whisper and the unexpected campsite cause me to creep as I cross the open ground to look at it. It feels like the trees have eyes, and I am an intruder. I peer at the laptop and gasp.

"What?" Sadie can't resist even though she also looks up at the trees as she reaches me. "Is that a picture of me?"

We lean in closer, shifting so the sun's glare isn't so strong on the screen. "It sure is!"

It's a night-vision photo of Sadie, Zenya, and the others with their arms full of plastic and glitter tubes. The screen flashes onto another photo. I see Ethan in the same strange lighting with his face painted, slipping into the girls' cabin. If I try hard enough, I can make out my face as I stand guard.

"Listen!" Sadie clutches my arm. I hear nothing, but I know not to question her keen ears. "Hide!"

She doesn't have to tell me twice with the strangeness of this place settling down on us. I rush for a bush which I'm thankful isn't thorns, but it proves plenty sharp as I dive into it like it's the deep end of a pool. The branches snap, far too loud in the heavy air, but at least the leaves close in around me like a shield.

"*Pssst!* Your boot!" Sadie whispers harshly.

Cringing, I pull my foot closer, but now even I can hear the quiet tread of footsteps. *Crack.* I freeze with the tip of my boots still sticking out, but I dare not move as a heavyset, balding man strides into the clearing, adjusting his belt. He goes straight to the laptop and shuts it off. After rummaging in his tent for a while, he emerges with a notebook clamped under his elbow.

He shoves a water bottle into a hiking pack and straps it on. The motion makes him drop the notebook. A paper flutters out, but he scoops up the book without seeing it. He sets off down a barely visible trail, and I breathe for the first time in two minutes. I count off 60 seconds that drag on forever.

Sadie eases out of her bush at the same time, and we rush for the piece of paper. She reaches it first, so I look over her shoulder. I see a tight handwritten script, but I don't get far past the large letters at the top that say, *"front-page article: Generation Alpha Is Going Down the Tubes."*

"Sadie, quit shaking the paper." I cover her hand

and find she's trembling. I snatch the paper closer when I see both Sadie's name and mine. At the bottom, the page is initialed with "E.Z."

"It seems today's youth know no boundaries as they wage a private war," I read, horrified.

"Is that man a newspaper writer?" she squeaks.

"You mean a *journalist*?"

"Whatever! This is awful! He has pictures of us, and everything…" She's getting frothed up quickly.

"He can't know we've been here. That means," I carefully tug the paper from her white-knuckled grip. "We leave this here. He will be sure to come back looking for it." The paper flutters to the ground.

"Come on! We've got to get out of here fast. Let's get back to the river and find Camp Wilderness; we can't be far away." I turn and start back the way we came. "Sadie, come on!"

But she's frozen in place, one hand still in front of her face as if she's still holding the paper. I race back and guide her forward by her elbow.

- 21 -

Turns out, we're not even 40 yards from where Camp Wilderness meets the river. We couldn't miss it anyway because of all the rafts pulled up on shore. Across the wide yard dotted with huge trees, a group of people have gathered. Blue police lights are flashing off the worried faces of the counselors.

"Hurry! What if somebody was hurt in the rapids?" Sadie rushes forward. Zenya is the first one to see her. She shrieks her name and then starts to cry.

I bite my tongue, and worry rises at her reaction. I scan the crowd for Ethan, but I don't see him. The blood drains from my face. Caroline's eyes are red from crying. *This doesn't look good.*

The group turns toward us as we hurry forward. Jim makes a strange sound in his throat when he sees us; then he hits the ground like a fallen log. Half the group gathers around us, and the other half surrounds Jim, who's groaning on the ground.

They fire questions at us, but I'm still searching for Ethan. Finally, I shout over the clamor of voices. "Where's Ethan?"

Dan shrugs. "He's in the bathroom."

I nearly faint with relief—just as Jim had. Sadie is right by my side. She doesn't budge—even though Zenya tries to pull her away. A door slams, and Ethan steps out.

"Oh, hey, y'all," he says easily. "You two have all the adventures. Next time I'm jumping ship too."

He wraps us in a hug with his long arms. Jim is there now, wiping tears from his eyes.

"What's wrong?" Sadie asks.

"We didn't figure there was any way you two could survive those rapids. I kept imagining having to tell your parents." He swipes at his face again, and I must admit that I like Jim even more than I did before.

"Hey, I bet you're thirsty! Come check this out." Ethan leads us over to our branches, which still look strange with our bags tied over them.

"Ethan, so help me, tell me right now if anybody else got hurt," Sadie says.

"Nope, just you two. Aaron bruised his leg, but he's all right. You sure have a habit of popping up like gophers when we least expect it."

"*Pop!*" Sadie says with a jump. Now that she knows everyone is all right, her silliness is back.

I flick the top corner of my foggy bag and watch the water droplets collect at the bottom. I pull the bag carefully off the tree and tilt it toward my mouth. There isn't much water inside, and it's hot and tastes…green somehow. But it sure soothes my dry throat.

"The heat of the sun caused the moisture in the leaves to condense, and our bags caught it," Ethan explains.

Sadie wipes her mouth after draining her bag. "That wasn't nearly enough. But I guess even that little bit would keep you from dehydrating or even dying in a survival situation."

Zenya hands her a tall, metal water bottle. Sadie pushes the button on top and starts chugging. Her eyes get wider and wider as she drinks faster.

"Zenya, what's in that bottle?"

"Sprite."

I leap forward and knock the bottle to the ground.

"Hey! That wasn't nice!" Sadie says in an annoyed tone. Then I watch the sugar take over. Her pupils get bigger, and a wide grin covers her face.

"Oops!" Zenya says, "I forgot she does that."

"Everybody, move slowly," Ethan orders, inching closer. "Now!"

He and I leap forward, but Sadie is long gone by the time we crash into each other.

"Yipeeeee!" She's halfway across the field by the time I'm back on my feet.

"Not again!" The counselors glance from Sadie, to me, to each other with horrified expressions.

"Catch her!" I shout.

Jim is still woozy from fainting when he saw us. The thought warms my heart even as I dash down the field, trying to ignore the blisters from hiking in soaked shoes. In fact, they're still squeaking right now. Sadie's sprint makes Caroline's top speed look like a tortoise.

"Oh, please, no!" I pant as Sadie disappears into the underbrush. Her scream makes my hair stand on end. Then a man's shout echoes her scream, and Sadie pops back out of the bushes, hands waving over her head, screaming at the top of her lungs.

I bet she spooked our mystery journalist! But I don't have the time to spend on that situation. Sadie has evaded yet another counselor's grasp and has now leaped on top of a car in the parking lot.

She does a flying front flip onto the next one, falls through its open sunroof, then explodes out the driver's door shouting, "I'm a monkey!"

Ethan laughs so hard he trips, which leaves Aaron and me at the front of the pack, chasing her.

"Monkey! Hey! I'm talking to you!" I shout, desperate to slow her down.

She turns with that crazed grin, *"Ooo-ooo-eee!"* She pumps her legs, knees out wide as she swings her arms like an ape.

Aaron signals, then veers around the cars, ducking low, so she doesn't see him coming. I slow down too, my hands wide and low as I creep up on her. "Easy now, monkey, I'm not going to hurt you."

Aaron bursts around the back of the car and swipes at Sadie's arm, missing by a mile. She leaps straight up onto the roof of the next car from a standstill.

"Wow!" Aaron whispers in awe. "I didn't think a person could do that."

She stares at Aaron with a stormy monkey face and argues in monkey talk: *"Eee-eee-ooohhhhh!"* In a flash she's off the cars, but Ethan materializes from nowhere and wraps her in a bear hug.

"*Eeee!*" she screeches. Sadie finally returns after another five minutes of "monkey wrestling."

"How did you jump clear onto that car?" Ethan asks.

"I didn't."

I just shake my head. "You met the mystery journalist too, didn't you?"

"The *who*?" Ethan wrinkles his nose.

Sadie tells him our story, then adds, "But I only saw him once—with you."

"No, I'm pretty sure you scared the daylights out of him when you took off into the woods, little monkey."

We investigate the area and sure enough, another handwritten paper is lying in the freshly churned boot prints.

"What's this?" Ethan asks, scooping it up. He gasps as he reads…

- 22 -

The kids attending Survival Week at Camp Wilderness seem more intent on destroying each other than learning bush-craft skills.

Ethan looks up at me. "Is this going in the newspaper?"

I shrug. "Whether it does or doesn't, the fact is, he's right. Ethan, the girls didn't wreck our cabin on Monday night."

Ethan growls, slamming his fist into the paper. "It was the Cabin 2 boys; I know it!"

"Ethan!" Sadie's exasperated tone makes him flinch. "The point is, look at what we've done to each other for no reason! This blowback is wrong, and it's got to stop!"

Ethan frowns. "But I've got the best prank ever planned for tonight."

She snatches the paper. "Look at what everyone else sees! Ethan, is this what you really want?"

Ethan squints as he continues to read:

Every generation has its troublemakers, but today's youth are surely the worst. Can America survive Gen Alpha?

He heaves a sigh. "But it's a fantastic prank."

"Ethan!" I scold.

He holds up his hands. "Okay! Okay! You're right. Maybe we did go too far."

"Too far?" I question. "We should have taken the hot pepper lemonade like men and responded with kindness." The idea hadn't crossed my mind until it came out of my mouth. It's what my dad would have done, and I could kick myself for having failed to act like him.

"So, we agree. The prank war stops now," Sadie declares.

"Umm, we might have a minor problem…"

"Such as what, Ethan?"

"The other boys know the plan."

"Well, you'll have to stop them," Sadie says.

"*Stop Aaron?* It would be easier to hold back a river with my hands!" I say.

By the time we are building our nightly campfire, we have failed to convince anyone else to call a truce—not Zenya, not Dan, and certainly not Aaron. To make matters worse, Ethan won't tell us what the prank is. *It must be a terrible one.*

I pull Sadie aside right before curfew. "Listen, stay alert. I have a bad feeling about tonight."

"Me too." Her eyes are wide in the firelight.

"Let's meet at 10:30. Maybe one of us will know more by then."

She hugs me. "Thanks, Isaiah."

By 10:00 p.m., Aaron, Dan, and Miguel have applied their camo face paint, and they're loading backpacks with orange Kool-Aid powder. I creep along behind them with every intention of sabotaging their efforts. Ahead we hear a rustle in the bushes, so we hit the damp ground and freeze. The rustling continues, getting closer. *Is it Sadie?*

A familiar, low growl sounds, and Aaron shifts.

"Hello again," Ethan whispers to the sound.

The growl ramps up to an all-out snarl, and I can hear the approaching crunch of footsteps.

"Run!" Dan shouts.

We are up in a heartbeat and flying through the dark. We reach the cabin in no time flat.

"See," Ethan pants, "my alter ego, the cougar, says we shouldn't go either."

I leave Ethan to deal with the boys and slip off to meet Sadie, giving the clump of bushes between our cabins a very wide berth.

"*Psst.*"

I center in on the sound. "Thank God the bobcat scared off the boys again."

"Oh, really?" she replies.

"Yeah, this time it actually came after us."

"No, I mean, you didn't make it to our cabin?"

"No, not at all."

"Then I need you to come with me." I follow her through the dark until we're right next to the outer wall of Cabin 4.

"Listen," she whispers.

In the quiet darkness, a faint thunk sounds.

"Hear that? We've been thinking you guys were trying to scare us, but now I'm really scared. What is that noise?"

The other three girls creep out. "Sadie, the noise is back."

I hold back a laugh. "I think I know what it is. Look, here's a loose board."

They all lean in as I pull out my pocketknife and pry back the slab of wood. I click on my flashlight, and two beady eyes reflect the light.

"It's a mouse!" Zenya cries.

"And it's got a baby in its mouth!"

"It's no ordinary mouse," Sadie adds. "It's a New

ROCKY MOUNTAIN CHALLENGE

Mexico meadow jumping mouse. Look at that! She's making sure her species doesn't go extinct by adapting to an unfamiliar environment. The mystery of the creepy walls is officially solved. I just wish we could discover the story behind the mystery journalist as easily."

-23-

Friday

Friday morning dawns clear and hot, and Jim calls me away from breakfast.

"Um...am I in trouble?" I ask, swallowing hard as I follow him.

"No, sir. Well, let me rephrase that. We're going to *pretend* you're in trouble. Today is Wilderness First-Aid Day, and we pulled two names from a hat." Jim keeps his voice low as we wander through the cafeteria. *I wonder who the other camper is.*

"Sadie Rawlings. Follow me," Jim says with his hands behind his back. "It's so strange that I picked a brother and a sister."

Sadie's face goes white, but I smile at her to tell her it's all right. Every eye is on us as we follow Jim down the hallway. Sadie leans over and whispers, "E.Z.… Do you think those were his initials?"

"I knew a kid with the initials of E.Z. once. In fact, he's right…here." Jim points to a picture in the hallway of a group of campers posed in front of the Rocky Mountain National Park sign.

"Is that you?" Sadie asks.

"Ha! I sure was a scrawny little kid, wasn't I?" Jim says. "But that's E.Z. He took a lot of teasing for those initials. Plus, he was the only kid who never finished the final obstacle course."

Sadie and I study the picture. A chubby face with a big forehead and glasses is squinting at the camera on the far end of the row.

"That's him," I whisper. *This is getting weirder all the time.*

"You know E.Z.?" Jim asked.

"Not really, but he's camped out only a few hundred yards from here," I say.

Jim turns toward us. "That's strange…"

"Not as strange as the article he's writing about Camp Wilderness and us," Sadie adds.

Jim's face goes white, and I wonder if he's going to faint again.

"You okay, sir?"

"He's doing what?" Jim questions.

We fill him in on that part of our river adventure, and he becomes even paler.

"Maybe you should sit down," I say as we step into his office. Jim plunks into a chair and drops his head into his hands. "Tell you what, let's cover the plan for the first-aid hike; on our way out to hide you, let's make a pit stop at E.Z.'s camp."

According to our instructions, I am supposed to be severely dehydrated, and Sadie has a leg injury. The rest of the group is supposed to hike out to find us, administer first aid, and get us back to safety.

By the time Jim leads us from camp, his nervousness has greatly increased. "Now listen, let's just go nice and quiet. Show me your best survival sneaking skills," he says as we approach the hidden camp.

"Okay," we agree, but I must say we do a better job of displaying our sneaking skills than he does. He steps on a dead branch as soon as we can see E.Z.'s camp through the trees. Jim freezes. E.Z. cringes and scans the woods through his thick glasses. Eventually, he goes back to typing on his computer. Just when my feet are going to sleep from standing so still, the man stands to swat at an annoying fly a couple of times. He then gathers his gear, minus the lost paper.

I release a sigh and shift positions; the soreness from fighting the river sure hurts. Jim eases up to the log where the computer still sits. A small solar panel is charging it today.

A box in the corner of the screen says, "Uploading 72%," and the rest of the screen displays the finished article. The content doesn't present the campers of Camp Wilderness in a good light. I'm ashamed, knowing I had earned my place in the article through my actions.

The third paragraph is all about Jim, how he had been a bully in years past, and how he is now teaching the next generation to act even worse. The cutting words make my stomach turn.

Jim clamps his mouth shut and motions for us to leave E.Z.'s camp. He walks a long way to the place where we are supposed to wait for the first-aid hikers to reach us.

Sadie chews her lip, and I shrug at her, unsure of what to do. Jim stares off into the woods with a faraway look in his eyes.

Finally, he releases a harsh breath. "The worst part is what E.Z. wrote is true."

Sadie and I stare at each other in shock. "What's true?" she whispers.

Jim shakes his head. "I never thought of myself as a bully. But looking at it through his eyes, he has every right to see it that way." Jim eases down onto a fallen log, and his entire story floods out.

"My first Wilderness Survival Week, we were the Wolves of Cabin 1. We won every competition. Cabin 5 came in last every single time. Eugene Zinder was…well…you saw the picture. He was easy to pick on. We thought it was fun and that he could handle it, you know? If he didn't want to be that way, then he would've changed." He makes a touching sound in his throat.

"All these years, how I treated him has been eating away at him, tearing him down. *Ugh*. I didn't mean it that way." His head drops into his hands again, and he falls silent.

"Maybe you could change it," Sadie suggests.

"What?" He looks up as if just seeing us for the first time.

"It's not too late. Eugene is right here…" She looks around and adds, "…somewhere."

Jim scowls, brooding as the minutes drift past.

-24-

"There they are!" Ethan's excited cry reaches us. I lie down and pretend to be semicomatose. Sadie holds her leg.

"Great job!" Caroline tells the group as they crowd around us. "Now, tell me what's wrong with Sadie and Isaiah."

I groan and try to roll over.

"We should check Isaiah by pinching the skin on the back of his hand. If it stays up in a little wrinkle, then we'll know he's dehydrated."

Somebody pinches my hand hard. "Ouch!"

"Easy," Caroline says. "For now, let's pretend that his skin stayed up in a little ridge."

"I've got electrolyte powder," Ethan says, adding two packets of bright-blue powder to a bottle of water. They force me into a sitting position, and Ethan puts the bottle to my lips.

"*Blah!*" I spit out the liquid. "It's too strong!"

Caroline laughs. "Okay, how about your other patient?"

It's after lunch by the time we get back from our hike, and Sadie and I are thankful to return to normal. The sharp ring of the emergency bell makes me jump up and locate Sadie right away. *Whew, she's not swinging from it this time. Wait… If that bell is ringing, there really is an emergency!* Every single camper rushes toward the field, gathering under the bell. As I look around, I see worry written on every face.

Jim is there, steadily pulling the rope with his muscular arms. Finally, he stops, and we all stare at him.

"Jim?" Caroline questions.

"I…" He clears his throat. "I learned something

today that, well, it's worth ringing every alarm bell we've got." As he speaks, his voice gets stronger and more confident. "Everyone, take a seat. I have a story to tell you."

"When I was your age, I came to Survival Week too." He shares his and Eugene's story so well that it's like I'm there, watching it unfold.

"I never thought much of it after that…until today. You see, Eugene is here, camping not far away, and he's drafted an article about this camp and me and some of you that I would really like to change." He clears his throat and swipes a forearm across his brow.

"I realized something else today too. I've been letting you all walk the same path that I did—only now I see how destructive it is to compete to the point that you're willing to possibly harm someone else physically, emotionally, or in any way."

The other four boys from my cabin squirm nervously, and I wonder about the orange Kool-Aid caper they had been planning.

"So, I am here to say that the pranks must stop. I know it all started in fun, but something like that can hurt both you and others. Are we all agreed?"

All around the circle we nod solemnly.

"Good. Now, I have something I'm going to need your help with. Caroline, don't we have a stack of poster boards in the storage shed?"

- 25 -

For a group of 30 people, we move quietly down the faint trail toward Eugene's camp. Jim holds the stack of poster boards against his chest, so they won't rattle and make more noise.

I hold up my fist, and everyone stops. Just like we planned, Jim hands me the first poster. I hold it so the handwriting is facing out.

Jim nods once with determination in his eyes. I step into the small clearing without a word. Eugene jumps up from his folding chair, pushing his glasses higher on his nose. His mouth opens, but he's too befuddled to speak. I watch his eyes read my sign.

We're sorry.

I step to the side, and Zenya walks out as silent as can be. I watch Eugene read her poster with an even more shocked expression.

For everything you went through as a kid.

We step aside, and the kids just keep coming one after another. Each one has a new message until Eugene is surrounded by posters. I glance around the circle.

I wish I could've been your friend.

You are important.

I won't prank anymore.

Jim had asked each of us to write something to Eugene, and it turned into a beautiful story.

I would have sat with you at lunch.

Eugene's eyes are soon red-rimmed, and then Jim steps out. Eugene shrinks back a little, but his eyes drop to the sign that Jim is holding.

Will you forgive me?

Eugene and Jim both blink back tears. When

Jim's voice breaks the long silence, it's even more powerful.

"Eugene, I never meant to hurt you. But I did, and I am so sorry. I had no right to treat you like I did."

Eugene's hand covers his mouth. I hold my breath until he says. "I don't…I don't know what to say."

What if he refuses? I bite the inside of my lip, hating what it would do to Jim when he's humbled himself so much. I'd admired him from the moment we met; but now with the way he's responded to the situation, he seems like a hero to me.

Eugene's voice squeaks. "Are you serious?"

Jim nods and seeing tears in his eyes is one of the manliest things I've ever seen.

"Well, of course I for…forgive you." Eugene seems to shrink even further into himself.

Caroline steps forward, biting her lip. "I was there that year too. I'm sorry I didn't stick up for you when I could have." She hurries forward and wraps Eugene in a hug. He can't seem to get a whole word out of his mouth.

"We would love to have you at our campfire tonight," Jim says.

I think I learned more about survival in those last few hours than I did all week.

-26-

Saturday

I wave to Mom and Dad sitting in the bleachers. We're now in a part of camp we haven't seen until this morning. They smile and wave back at me. I hadn't realized how much I missed them until they had wrapped me in a hug.

Jim puts his megaphone to his mouth. "In a few hours, Wilderness Survival Week will be over."

The statement brings a groan of disappointment from all the campers. It's truly been one of the best weeks of my life.

"You're going home as Rocky Mountain National Park Junior Rangers, equipped with the knowledge to keep both yourselves and others alive in the wilderness." He pauses, and I know he's thinking about last night.

"We've all learned a lot, and I hope you are leaving as better people."

I wish I could hug him and tell him thanks for teaching us how to act like real men.

"But first, you've got to complete what we call… 'Big Bertha'—the toughest obstacle course this side of the Mississippi! The course will challenge your strength, agility, and smarts! So far, you have been competing as teams. But in this course, you'll be running individually. If you fall, get back up, go to the start of the obstacle, and try again. Who's ready?"

We shout long and loud, and my blood pumps fast as I look over the course. It's shaped like a U with the bleachers for the parents in the center.

We have no time to study the obstacles as the counselors position us at the starting line. Sadie stretches, pulling out the soreness from our raft experience. I find plenty of kinks in my own limbs.

Ethan is making whooshing sounds as he jumps around like a ninja.

"Ready, set..." Jim shouts, pointing a starting pistol skyward. "Go!"

The shot creates instant motion as we rush forward to a series of walls. I leap up and throw my leg over, only to find I've got to jump down into a ditch filled with mud. Beside me, Ethan leaps first, and mud splatters up into my face. I laugh and follow him, the cold, wet mud plopping everywhere.

Climbing the next wall with my slimy legs proves far more difficult. I know the exact second each of the four girls at camp hits the mud because they shriek loud and long.

I finally gain the top of the wall and flat out jump the last wall. We've spread out now, each camper finding his or her own pace.

Ahead are log teeter-totters, and the wood is slick with no bark to grip. Ethan rushes up one, his arms stretched wide, striving for balance. He gets to the tipping point as I start up another.

"Whoa!" He stretches one leg forward, trying to get the log to shift without bucking him off. It moves; but when the high end hits the ground, it nearly throws him off. I'm not entirely sure how he manages to stay on, but now he's running down the far side.

I work on tilting my log, but when it slams down, both my feet slide off. I end up dangling by my hands, and the wide log is hard to grip.

Zenya, then Aaron, finish the teeter-totters, pushing forward after Ethan.

"Come on!" I shout to myself, climbing hand over hand down to the far end. I rush forward, studying the wall head. Ethan has short loops of rope in each hand, and he's flinging them onto knobs that are bolted to the wall.

I pull two ropes from the pile, ignoring the dripping sweat and mud. I get up two knob heights, and then Sadie's next to me. She's better at flicking the loops up onto a higher knob and making them catch. I try twice more till mine finally hooks. Now

I can use my feet to climb as well, and it goes faster. Sadie reaches the top, turns to one side, tucks her legs up, and uses her momentum to somersault over the top.

"Hey, you monkey!" I tease.

She gives a wild laugh. *"Eee-eee-ohhhh!"*

I gain the top and find a steep slide down the other side. I hit the ground running. Ahead is another steep bank without a speck of grass on it. It looks like the counselors had run a hose over it for hours to create a mud pit. Ethan, Aaron, and Zenya are halfway up, but Aaron loses what grip he had and takes out the other two as he falls. They look like mud monsters writhing in the muck.

Zenya goes wild, wrestling with Aaron. "Leave me alone!" she shouts as mud flings everywhere.

I shake my head. Some people just never learn. I body slam into the hill, scrambling wildly up the slick slime. *"Grrr!"* Fighting gravity takes all my determination as I make slow progress, going in reverse more than forward.

Ethan and Zenya finally gain the top, and Sadie is right behind them. Aaron can't seem to get up the second time.

I wipe mud from my face when I'm finally at the top, but that makes it worse. Four smaller zip lines run from the top of the dam down into the center of the pond. Caroline stands to one side, waiting to pull back the handles for the next group of competitors to use.

Ethan grabs the simple inverted T-shaped handle and poises to push off. But then he looks over at Zenya, who is staring pale-faced at the drop-off. He sighs, standing up straight again. "Listen, Zenya. Just don't look down; focus straight ahead."

"No. No, I can't," she stammers.

Ethan's eyes narrow. "But you *could* mastermind one side of the most epic prank wars in history."

She rolls her eyes with a hint of a smile. "You bet I could."

He thrusts his chin at her. "Then surely, you are not going to let this little zip line stop you."

She shrugs weakly. Sadie and I grab the other two handles.

"Yeah, Zenya, you can do it," I encourage.

"I'll be right beside you," Sadie offers.

Zenya's eyes flick to Ethan's. "Okay. I'll do it if you'll do a trust fall."

"Oh…" Ethan says, his top lip pulled up. "You drive a hard bargain, Missy."

"Sure do." She cocks her hip.

"Fine. I'll do it. Now come on."

She reaches forward, fingers trembling as she holds her breath. It feels good to be all together.

"One, two, three!" Sadie shouts, and we push off. Zenya's breath comes out in the loudest scream I believe I have ever heard. The handles quickly hit the end of the zip line. The sudden stop rips our grips loose, and we flip through the air, spinning like wild. I perform a huge belly flop. *Will I get extra points for that landing?* We come up laughing, swimming hard for the shore.

"That was great!" Zenya giggles.

I feel heavy as I scramble out of the pond. Ahead is another wall that is way too high to climb. Behind us I hear the zip lines run again. *I had better hurry!*

The bottom of this wall is about three feet off the ground; I duck low, peering underneath. A long runway of muck stretches out ahead with a rope net hanging a foot or two from the surface.

"Looks like an army mud crawl," I say. I slam onto my stomach and inch forward on my knees and elbows. Ethan is like a snake sliding along as he outpaces the rest of us, and now Aaron is beside me too. Mud is in every crevice, and we look like swamp creatures emerging from the shadows. Passing out from under the net, I stand up, panting hard as I study the final obstacle.

Ethan is far ahead, easily climbing a rope ladder that leads to a platform. The tall pole it's built on is surrounded by more mud. His feet hit the wooden platform, and he gives out a whoop of victory. All he has to do is run across, climb one more wall, and then cross the finish line. He darts forward, throwing his arms high as he strikes a pose. "I WIN! Uh-oh." I hear a sudden screech as the platform tilts to one side. Arms cartwheeling, Ethan shouts as he falls, *"I loossseeee!"* The mud on his shirt and pants helps him slide straight toward the moat.

Now Aaron is on the platform. "Whoa…" He jigs to one side, trying to keep it from tilting back and forth. It works for a second, but he can't scramble back fast enough to recover it. He makes a big smack as he lands next to Ethan. More kids reach the rope ladder, clogging up at the bottom.

We all try the platform, but there is no way to cross it! Aaron and Zenya try it together.

"Stop it! You're going to make me fall."

"You're going to do that, anyway!" Then they both slide off into the mud.

But their failure gives me an idea. "Sadie!" She's about to climb the rope net for another try. "Wait."

She comes over, solid brown with mud, only her eyes are bright.

"Do I look as funny as you?"

"Yep." She smiles, "What's up?"

"Let's try it together."

"That didn't work so well for Zenya and Aaron."

"Yeah, but we are not them. Hold on." We wait while Dan and Miguel fail and splat next to the rest of the kids. Getting free from the deep, churned mud takes a while, and everyone is currently stuck.

"Now!" We rush forward and climb. "I'm heavier than you, so I'll have to stay closer to the center. You'll be the counterweight as we keep pace with each other!"

"Right." She looks at me and nods. We step onto the mud-covered platform.

"Easy now…" I hold out a hand as the platform tilts my way. "Go farther out!"

She steps away from me, and the platform levels, creaking ominously.

"Okay, we're good. Step forward," she says. As we slide our right legs forward together, the platform groans, and we freeze.

"Again," she says.

This time my leg slides crazily on the mud, and I go down hard to one knee. The platform jumps, Sadie screeches, scrambling for balance.

I don't breathe, arms wide, completely focused. "I'm going to stand up."

"Slowly," she whispers.

Two more steps forward, and we look at each other. "Jump!" we shout, launching for the solid section of platform straight ahead. We roll to a stop on the firm area, laughing.

"Nice work, Rawlings kids!" Jim grins at us. "That is the fastest anyone has ever conquered Big Bertha. You've reached the last obstacle, who is going to win?" *He's expecting us to fight it out.*

"Come on, Sadie," I say as we approach the wall, but it's too high to climb. We search for another way or tools—*anything.*

I turn to Jim. "It's impossible. There's no way to reach the top."

He shrugs. "You've got each other."

I look over at Sadie, nodding. After all, it's her turn to win.

"I'll boost you over," she says, obviously thinking the same thing.

"A little monkey like you is going to boost *me* over this wall?"

She frowns up at it with her hands on her hips. "Maybe not," she admits.

"Come on. We don't have any time to waste." I swallow down the sour taste of losing and cup my hands together like a step.

"You're the best brother ever!" she declares. I hoist her high, and she wiggles into a sitting position on the top of the wall. "Here, I'm going to help you up." Then she slides around until her legs are hanging over the far side.

"Sadie, just go. The finish line is right there."

"Not without you," she answers in a stern tone.

"Fine. I'll prove to you that you can't get me up and over this wall."

I grab her hands and even though she pulls for

all she's worth, I don't get far. Our muddy grips slip, and I slam back to my feet.

"Go on, Sadie! Hurry!"

"No!"

"What are you going to do? Let everyone run right past you?" I growl. Ethan and Zenya have paired up, trying our trick on the platform; but they lose it and fall.

"Yes."

"Ugh. Come on, Sadie, don't make me do this."

"Do what?"

I pull a smashed candy bar from my back pocket. It's covered in mud, and I frown at it for a while, chewing the inside of my cheek. The way I see it is this: one-half bar equals a *raving maniac*. One-quarter bar equals *completely crazy*. One bite equals *turbo speed*.

"Are you sure about this, Isaiah?" Jim asks.

"According to my careful calculations, it should give her just enough energy to boost me up."

"Seems risky to me," he hedges.

Rocky Mountain Challenge

I snap off half a bite and toss it up to her. Jim crouches, ready to catch her.

"That's all?" she whines.

"Yep." I stuff the rest in my mouth.

"Fine." She pops it in and chews. "Yum." Then her eyes get brighter.

"Take it easy," Jim says, nervously.

"Now!" I reach up and she grunts, straining. I throw one leg over the top. "I'm…up!"

"*Wahoo!*" She grabs my hand as we jump down and run across the finish line together.

-27-

We're all cleaned up, sitting in the big dining hall with all the parents at the back. Once all of us campers had finally finished Big Bertha, Jim and Eugene had run the course. We had all cheered like crazy when they crossed the finish line together. Eugene had sheepishly admitted to ransacking our cabins to start the prank war. After getting over the shock, it became our turn to forgive him.

"I'd like to let you all know I've decided not to run the article," Eugene says, and I sag in relief. Honestly, I don't think survival training camp could have turned out any better.

Jim is now standing at the front with the rest

of the counselors. "It's my privilege to present our survival training awards. Each award is given for exceptional behavior, skill, or courage."

Maybe Sadie will receive the award for the wildest camper.

"First, I would like to invite the campers from Cabin 3 to the stage."

My face gets red as we step forward.

"Your cabin came in first in overall points for the week, with Cabin 2 and Cabin 3 for a close second and third."

All the parents clap, but I find I don't really want the fancy award with my name on it. I'm only too glad to sit back down. But Aaron and Ethan dance their way back down the aisle.

"Now for the personal awards. The first one is the Biggest Overcomer. This award recognizes an exceptional effort of bravery in conquering a fear. Zenya, please come to the stage. We applaud you for accomplishing your second try at a zip line."

We all clap and whistle as she accepts the award.

"Next is the Biggest Goofball Award. Each year, without fail, one camper shines forth as the most popular, the silliest, and the funniest kid. Ethan, please step on up!"

Ethan jumps up with a whoop, then dances his way to the front. As he takes the award, a kid shouts, "Ethan, sign my face!" And with that, Ethan is working his way back to his seat, signing people's faces and shirts with a black permanent marker.

Sadie shakes her head. "Only Ethan."

"All right, all right." Jim holds his hands up in the air. "The final award, Most Likely to Survive, is a big award that belongs only to those who have shown an extra measure of courage, ingenuity, and skill. It's my honor to present it to…Isaiah Rawlings."

I sit there, wondering who is going to get up. Ethan slaps my shoulder. "Go on, man! That's you!"

"What?"

Sadie stands up, clapping and cheering. "That's my brother!"

In a daze, I stand up and somehow find myself on stage. Jim shakes my hand.

"Isaiah Rawlings, it's been an honor to watch you turn back to help others who weren't even on your team, to selflessly rescue your sister, and to offer to give up your winning position in the final race. It's a privilege to know you." He pulls me into a hug, and I swallow back tears. All those instances he had mentioned had only been the right thing to do—plain and simple.

I look out over the crowd. Sadie is clapping and jumping in place. I sure wish I hadn't been so quick to accuse her, but I'm glad we got the situation all straightened out. Even if the girls had wrecked our cabin, I'm still the one who chose how to respond. And next time, I will act more like my dad and like Jim on the obstacle course conquering Big Bertha with Eugene.

- 28 -

It's nearly time to leave camp, so I lift Sadie's bag off her bunk in the girls' cabin. "What have you got in here? Bricks?"

She shrugs, helping Zenya get her suitcase zipped. "It was a whole week away from home; I needed a lot of stuff."

"Oh, look! Chocolate sprinkles!" Ethan says, reaching for a trail of small brown pellets along the edge of a bunk. He scoops up a few and pops them into his mouth. His eyes go wide as he clutches his throat. *"Plwwph!"*

He spews out the pieces, spitting wildly, and making choking sounds. He ends up flat on the floor. "Water! Get me some water, please! I need to rinse out my mouth!"

I laugh and toss him a bottle. "Guess chocolate sprinkles and mouse poo really do look alike."

"You can be partially thankful it was from an endangered mouse species," Sadie adds.

Ethan just groans on the floor.

I haul Sadie's huge bag out the door, and everyone follows. Ethan heads off to the side, still spitting like crazy.

"Where do *you* think you're going?" Zenya asks, snapping her fingers. Ethan's face goes pale. "You thought I would forget about the trust fall, huh?"

"I sure had hoped so," he replies.

"Come on," she says. Aaron, Dan, Miguel, Sadie, Ethan, and I head toward the log. We link arms, ready to catch him as he climbs up on the stump.

He shakes out his hands. "I don't know about this. Are you sure you can catch me?"

"Oh, come on!" Aaron says.

"Don't you trust us by now?" Dan adds.

Ethan turns around, stiff as a board.

"We're right here, Ethan!" I encourage.

He lets out a short breath, screams like a girl, and then falls back. We easily cradle his weight. His clenched eyes snap open. "I survived!"

We laugh and joke about camp memories as we head back.

"Wait!" Sadie says, holding up a hand.

Our entire group freezes. Just ahead in the thick grass, I see movement.

"What is it?" Aaron whispers. Gray fur splotched with tan is moving!

"Kittens!" Sadie gasps.

"Not just *any* kittens," I add. "Those are *bobcat* kittens!" We watch the little furballs wrestle in the grass. "That's why the mama kept growling at us. She had babies to protect!"

"Wow!" Sadie breathes, completely in love. "They are so cute!"

"Hey!" Ethan shouts. "That's my hat!"

At his shout, a growl rattles the brush straight ahead, and the kittens scatter, leaving behind a rumpled and soaked coonskin cap.

"I bet Mama Bobcat slipped through the open door after Eugene left and ate my jerky. Then she snagged your cap, thinking it was a meal for her kittens!"

Ethan strides forward and dusts off his hat, a trail of slime on his hand.

"*Eww!*" Sadie grabs her nose. "It smells like kittens have used it for an outhouse!"

Ethan frowns at what used to be the fluffy tail at the back—now a little stub of spiky fur! He slaps it onto his head.

"Stinky or not, it's *my* hat, and I'm still gonna wear it!"

P.S.

Hey, Ethan here!

I know you are wondering what my super-amazing prank with the Kool-Aid is. But the thing is, C. R. Fulton told me it was so good that it's like top secret information. So, you'll just have to keep guessing!

See you in Grand Canyon Rescue. I can't wait!